Nine Holidays Falling

Erin Graves

To those who need a reminder that it's okay to slow down.
Life happens in all the little moments, not just the big ones.
Take time to appreciate all of them.

AUTHOR'S NOTE

Nine Holidays Falling is an open-door romance intended for mature readers, containing sexually explicit and adult content. While this story is filled with friends, family, and love, and a happily ever after is guaranteed, it does touch on some sensitive subjects. You can find a complete list in the back of the book or on my website.

www.eringravesauthor.com

PLAYLIST

"Auld Lang Syne" – The Hound + The Fox

"The New Year" – Death Cab for Cutie

"Elephant Love Medley" – Moulin Rouge Soundtrack

"St. Patrick's Day" – John Mayer

"Linger" – The Cranberries

"Still into You" – Paramore

"Halloween" – Noah Kahan

"The Good Part" – AJR

"All I Want for Christmas Is You" – Mariah Carey

"Boxing Day" – blink-182

"Hanging by a Moment" – Lifehouse

"The Christmas Song" – Nat King Cole

DECEMBER

CHAPTER ONE

Sadie

"IF IT ISN'T LITTLE Sadie Winslow," a smooth, familiar voice calls from behind me. "What are the chances of seeing you here?"

Part of me hates that I can identify that deep voice so easily—that I can hear the smirk that accompanies it. It's been three years since I've seen him, and yet I know exactly who it is without turning around.

As I twist to look at him, I'm unsurprised to find that smirk I so easily heard stretched across his lips.

"Reid Alexander." I try to hide the disdain in my voice, but his pinched brows tell me I'm unsuccessful. "I guess I shouldn't be surprised to see you here." It's harder than I imagine for my lips to form a smile, but I force it all the same.

I've always been a people pleaser, and hurting others—no matter how much they may deserve it—has never been something I enjoy.

He recovers quickly, his eyes brightening as he opens his arms wide. "This is my hometown," he croons, letting his arms fall to his sides as his gaze travels the length of my body. The heated look in his eyes as they trail over my wide-legged trousers and up my strapless corset top makes my skin tingle—and I hate it.

When I picked this outfit for the New Year's Eve party, I'd been hoping to draw the attention of an attractive man. It's been awhile since I've been with anyone, and being away from my normal small town crowd opened up more possibilities, but Reid Alexander wasn't even in the realm of possibility—he is not an option.

Ashford Falls, Maryland is just as small as my hometown, one where everyone knows everyone, but I assumed he wouldn't show his face at the same party my sister planned on attending. The chances of seeing him should have been slim.

I can admit the man is attractive. Piercing blue eyes that are almost gray. A square jaw lined with stubble. Tall and muscular. A smile that would melt the panties off any woman. All you have to do is look past his playboy tendencies and his rude behavior—how the man succeeds at getting so many women to sleep with him, I'll never know.

Okay, that's a lie…I know exactly how he does it.

Even knowing all I do about him, I can't stop my thighs from clenching at the spark of interest in his eyes—from the look my sister's ex-boyfriend is giving me as his gaze lingers on my cleavage.

How good would it feel to have his stubble rubbing against my chest as he lavished all his attention there? No. That is not a thought I'm allowed to have about my sister's ex. It wouldn't be right to think like that about any of her exes, but the one who broke her heart? The one who got away? I could never do that to her. She's always been my best friend, there for me when I need her.

I'm shocked by the images that flash in my mind. The moment I knew who Reid was, I couldn't look at him in a sexual way, and I can't believe I am now. Not that I'd ever act on them.

Even if he wasn't my sister's ex and was just some guy she knew, the stories she's told? I sometimes wonder how she was with him as long as she was.

"I guess I hoped and assumed you'd draw the short straw and be working this evening. Even in small towns, New Year's is a busy night for first responders." I cross my arms, but the flare of heat in Reid's eyes has me dropping them quickly, and I hate the burn I feel creeping up my cheeks. The hazards of being a redhead—you can never hide a blush.

"Well," he starts but pauses a moment, his eyes shifting over my shoulder as he visibly swallows before continuing. "You're half right"—his eyes meet mine and that smirk is back—"I am on call tonight. So, while I can't participate in all the festivities this evening, I can still come out and celebrate."

"And you choose the same party Summer's at?"

Anger flashes across his face at the mention of my sister, but it's gone so quickly I swear I imagined it. "If I avoided everywhere your sister might be I'd be stuck in my house for the rest of my life. You're no stranger to small town living." It's a half-hearted attempt at a joke, and we both know it.

While it's been three years since I've seen or spoken to Reid, there was a time I thought I knew him pretty well. Summer and I may have lived in different towns for the last six years, but luckily when she decided to leave our hometown of Stonebridge Hollow, Pennsylvania, she only moved a short thirty-minute drive to Ashford Falls.

When she announced she was moving, it shocked me, but after seeing the life she built for herself here, it became clear just how much she needed the change of scenery. Then Reid entered the picture, and everything really clicked into place. I honestly thought they were going to end up married, but after three years together, Summer broke up with him.

When she showed up at my doorstep with tears pouring down her cheeks, I was at a complete loss for words. They seemed so solid I couldn't understand what happened. But after hearing all the things Reid did, I don't know how they even made it six months together.

Then again, I never would have thought Reid capable of the things Summer had told me. Reid had shown himself to be a master manipulator, and I don't envy the position Summer has been in for the last two and half years since their breakup. I don't think I could live so close to the man who broke my heart, especially in a small town like Ashford Falls.

"There's a difference between avoiding Murphy's because there's a possibility Summer might be there and avoiding a party you know she's going to. This is her friend's house."

"Sadie." Reid laughs, but the sound is hollow. "We both know your sister wouldn't be caught dead in Murphy's." He pauses, almost like he wants to make sure his next word can't be missed. "It's not classy enough for her."

My brows pinch and I can't stop my eyes from falling to the ground. I want to argue with him, but we both know I can't. I love my sister more than anyone. We've always been there for each other, through all of our ups and downs, but the way Summer views the world around her has never made sense to me.

We didn't grow up in some privileged house where everything was given to us. Our parents taught us to work for the things we wanted in life, and that's what we did. But somewhere along the way, Summer developed a taste for the fancier side of life.

"There's nothing wrong with liking nice things," I mumble, forcing my gaze back to his.

"You're absolutely right. But Murphy's isn't trash."

Of course, Reid is right again. Murphy's is the one and only bar in Ashford Falls, and while I've only been there once or twice, it's probably my favorite place in town. The moment you walk into the bar it feels like coming home—everything about the place is warm and cozy. It doesn't hurt that the owner is there to greet you with a smile when you walk in.

But that means nothing to Summer.

She wants the sleek modern look. The kinds of places you see in Hollywood movies and TV shows. Her need for glitz and glam is one of the many reasons I don't understand why she still lives in Ashford Falls. Ever since Summer broke up with Reid, it seemed like she was outgrowing small town living. She seemed far more suited for the city life these days.

"No," I mutter. "Murphy's isn't trash."

Reid's brows pinch as he studies me, his eyes moving all over my face. Something like empathy fills his eyes, and I force myself to straighten my shoulders and clear all emotion from my face. I have no idea what he saw to give me that look, but I refuse to take any coddling from Reid Alexander.

"Still, you're a smart man, you knew the chances of Summer being here were high. I'm surprised you chose this party."

"Sweetheart." He smirks, taking a step toward me and cutting the space between us in half. I'm not sure if it's a move that's meant to intimidate me or not, but I refuse to step away.

My desperation to hold my ground has nothing to do with the fact I can feel the heat of him against my bare skin—not even a little bit.

"Your sister might have a lot of power over the people in her orbit, but I'll never give her that kind of power over me again."

Before I have a chance to speak, he lifts a hand, brushing a piece of hair behind my ear. The feel of his fingers against the skin of my neck stuns me silent. He doesn't say anything else as he lingers there for only a moment before he walks away.

I hate that I can still feel the ghost of his fingers hours later.

CHAPTER TWO

Reid

THE MOMENT I SAW Sadie Winslow across the room I knew I was in for a world of trouble. I couldn't take my eyes off of her.

No matter how many times I repeated in my head how terrible the idea was, I couldn't stop my feet from moving toward her. It was like some magnetic force was pulling me in.

Here's the thing about Sadie Winslow—she was never anything more than my girlfriend's little sister. I cared about her in the sense that I knew Summer loved her and wanted the best for her, but unless she was right in front of me, I didn't think about her.

Seeing her across the room at a friend's New Year's Eve party shouldn't have made me oblivious to everything else around me. If anything, seeing her should have made me think of the horrible human being she's related to. The one I'd seen only moments before who had me heading for the door before my attention was captured by the stunning redhead.

I want to say I didn't realize it was her when I first started moving toward her, but that would be a lie. I knew exactly who she was when I laid eyes on her. Her vibrant red hair would give her away in any crowd, but it was the radiant smile stretched across those red lips that pulled me in.

I'd waited until the woman she was talking to walked away before I approached, but instead of greeting her the way I would have greeted anyone else, I had to be an ass. Calling her Little Sadie Winslow had been my attempt at reminding me exactly who she was, but the moment I let my gaze roam her body…how had I missed truly seeing her before?

It's not really a mystery. I might have the reputation of a playboy, but I've never looked at another woman while in a relationship. Having been cheated on before, I'd never be able to cause that kind of pain to someone else.

And the truth of the matter is that I thought I was in love with Summer Winslow. Looking at another woman when I felt the way I did about her never even crossed my mind.

Falling in love with Summer—or so I thought—was easy.

She's magnetic and knows how to draw people in.

But she's also a manipulative bitch—or so I like to remind myself every time I think of her. If I let myself, I'll drown in my doubt. How I went three years blinded to who she really was I'll never understand—especially in my line of work.

Ten years on the force, and I didn't see the truth until it was too late.

Shaking myself from my thoughts I pull the Ashford Falls Police Department beanie onto my head before stepping out the door of the precinct. I wasn't supposed to be on patrol this evening, but being called in might be for the best.

It was hard enough walking away from Sadie when I did. Staying at the party and watching her wasn't an option, but that's exactly what I found myself doing. My gut told me Sadie is nothing like her sister, but I haven't trusted my gut in years.

The truth is, that call from Lyle—needing coverage for another officer who called out sick—couldn't have come at a better time. I needed her out of my line of sight.

I needed her out of my town.

I pause at the edge of the sidewalk and take a deep breath, letting my head fall back. My eyes fall closed as the cool night air pours into my lungs, and I wish I could say it smells like snow, but I'm out of luck.

My phone chimes and I dig it out of my pocket, finding a text from my friend and partner.

Gage: Thanks for taking the call tonight. I owe you one.
Reid: No you don't. You worked Christmas. It's my turn to take one for the team.
Reid: Now stop texting me and take a different one for the team.
Reid: Go get laid.
Gage: I wish. But I'm staying in tonight. No chance of getting laid here all by myself.
Reid: Remind me why I took this call for you? I was out trying to get laid.
Gage: Because you love me and wanted to give me a night of relaxation.
Reid: Oh, right. That sounds like something I would do.
Gage:
Gage: I appreciate you!
Reid: Yeah, yeah. Go enjoy that night of relaxation.
Gage: You know I will.

Locking my phone, I stuff it back into my pocket with a soft chuckle. Gage might think he's pulling a fast one on me, but I'm pretty confident his night of relaxation is actually a night in with that lawyer he met at the courthouse a few months ago.

I can't be sure—he hasn't told me anything—but I know he's been spending less and less time out and around town when he's not on shift, and I know he's had dinner with her at Murphy's almost every Thursday since she landed in town. For a man who's never seen with the same woman more than twice, that's pretty significant.

My gut says there's something serious brewing between Gage and Ava, but it's also led me astray before.

Taking one more deep breath, I stuff my hands in the pockets of my jacket to fight off the cold and start my walk down Main Street. There are a few stragglers rushing down the street to make it into either Murphy's or The Diner just in time for the clock to strike midnight, but for the most part, the street is empty.

With only a few minutes left until New Year's Day officially arrives, I don't expect to see anyone, especially not a lone figure standing in the gazebo in the center of town. Even from this distance, I know exactly who it is and I know I should continue my trek down the street and away from her, but just like at the party, I'm drawn to her.

I clear my throat a few feet before my steps hit the gazebo, wanting to make sure she knows someone is close. I may be confused about what's going on with me and my feelings toward Sadie, but I don't want to scare her.

"What are you doing here?" The words are soft, floating on the crisp air.

"I needed some fresh air." Her gaze stays focused on the night sky, almost as if she's looking for something.

"The town gazebo isn't necessarily close to the party I left you at." My shoulder brushes hers as I step up to her side. I know I'm closer than I should be, but when she doesn't shift away from me, I decide I'm exactly where I should be.

"No, I guess it's not." She shifts slightly, turning her body to face me, and I can't help myself from studying her in the silence between us.

There's no denying Sadie is a beautiful woman—one who, had it not been for our history, I wouldn't have hesitated in flirting with. There's no question her red hair grabs everyone's attention. It's the kind of red that catches fire every time the sun shines on it—the kind that's clear to see is 100 percent natural. But her high cheekbones and well-defined jawline are just as gripping. There's an elegance to her that can't be ignored, and the sunburst of gold in her hazel eyes holds me captivated.

"I love my sister," Sadie murmurs, her voice bringing me back to the moment. "But I won't lie. She's never been very good about remembering to make sure those around her feel included, especially when they don't really know anyone else."

"No, I can't say she ever has." My words are hushed and the stillness of the world around us creates this little bubble that neither of us are willing to pop.

"You were always so quiet when you visited Stonebridge with her."

"I was."

"At first I thought it was because you were uncomfortable around us, but after you two broke up I figured it was because you were an asshole." The words are said so quietly and calmly, it takes me a second to register them, but she doesn't give me a chance to say anything before she continues. "Now I'm not so sure that's what it was."

"You think I'm an asshole?" It's not the question I really

want to ask, but it's the first thing out of my mouth anyway.

"Oh, sweetheart." She smirks, her words clearly chosen to mock me. "I *know* you're an asshole. I just don't know if that's why you're a different person here in your hometown versus my hometown."

If it were any other woman, I may have been able to get my bearings before she pats my cheek twice and spins away from me, marching off into the night just as the muffled cheers of "Happy New Year" reach me in the center of town.

But she's not any other woman. She's my ex-girlfriend's younger sister, and even though she just called me an asshole, I find her more intriguing than I ever thought possible.

Yeah. Sadie Winslow is a beautiful woman, but my gut is telling me her soul is equally as beautiful. I just hope I can trust it.

FEBRUARY

CHAPTER THREE

GOING ON A BLIND date on *Valentine's Day. What could possibly go wrong?*

I don't know how Madison convinced me to go on this date, but if making the trek out to Gettysburg, Pennsylvania wasn't enough to make me second-guess this decision, not looking up the restaurant before I drove here definitely is.

"Madison," I hiss into the phone. "What in the world have you gotten me into?"

"What?" She laughs. "It sounded like a good time. Plus, I figured it was a safer choice."

"A communal dining experience? So instead of having dinner with one stranger I have to deal with a whole table full?" I hear the hysteria building in my voice and take a second to center myself.

I've never been more thankful for my overplanning tendencies. My inability to handle getting anywhere less than five minutes before I'm supposed to be there has never come in more handy than this moment.

The moment I walked up to the restaurant and saw the kind of place it was, I called Madison. I love her dearly—she's been my best friend since we were little—but this is so far out of the norm for her, I don't have words.

"Think of it more like a line of tables for two with no gap in between them. Sure, you'll be sitting next to strangers who are on dates, but no one will expect you to talk to them."

"Did you pick this place or did what's-his-name pick it?"

"Sadie." She sighs. I can imagine her sitting at the front desk of her family inn, patiently waiting for someone to check-in or have a question about something to do in town. It hurts my heart knowing she was supposed to be out on her own date but her boyfriend had to cancel due to some work thing. And now, instead of being out having a good time, she's there alone. "His name is Christopher, you know that."

"Yeah, but Christopher sounds so formal. Why not go by Chris?"

"Look, you were the one who wanted a date for Valentine's. I got you one, with a guy I genuinely think you'll like. Just…" Her words trail off and I hear the exasperation in her tone. "Just try to have a good time."

"Sorry," I mumble, falling back against the wall behind me. "You're right. I should be more open-minded."

"I love you. Give me a call when you're on your way home."

"I will. Love you too."

"Wow. That's pretty big to say to someone you've only been with for a little over a month." That smooth, deep voice I haven't stopped thinking about since New Year's sounds from my side, making me jump. "Sorry, didn't mean to startle you."

I wish I could say that apology wasn't authentic, but I see the emotion painted across his face in the slight frown and pinched brows as I turn to look at him, slipping my phone back into my purse. I kind of hate I can read that so easily—

and that it softens me toward him slightly.

This man broke my sister's heart.

While I thought he was one of the good ones, he turned out to be just like every other man. This fluttery feeling growing in my stomach needs to cut it out. It isn't right, whatever it is.

"What in the world are you doing here?" I huff.

Why does he have to look so good?

There's nothing all that unique about his appearance. It's clear he styled his dark hair and trimmed his beard this morning, and he probably took time to think about his outfit, but under the pea coat it's just a simple dark sweater worn with a pair of charcoal gray slacks. Nothing outstanding…and yet, I can't stop my eyes from wandering.

And of course, the asshole has to catch me.

"I assume the same thing you're doing here—a date." While there's a smirk stretched across Reid's lips, it's not nearly as condescending as I'd expect. "Though, my date clearly isn't as serious as yours. It's only a first date."

My eyes fall shut, and while I'm not sure I believe in God, I still find myself praying to him. "Why, oh why, is this my life?" I mutter under my breath.

"It's not that bad." Reid chuckles.

I peek one eye open, hoping he'll have disappeared somehow, but luck is not on my side. "I think it is," I say, slumping against the side of the building again.

"Sadie?" a cool voice asks from my other side, making me jump yet again.

"That's me." I smile, turning my back on Reid and taking in the man before me. He's not unattractive, but nothing about him causes the kind of reaction I had to seeing Reid just a few minutes ago, or even last month. "Christopher?" I ask, making sure this is the man I'm supposed to be meeting.

Madison described him as tall with light brown hair and a chin dimple—like a young Robert Mitchum.

Did I have to go home and look up who Robert Mitchum was after she said that? Yeah, I did.

I love my best friend, but her obsession with old movies isn't something the two of us share. I'll have to give her this one, though—Christopher definitely looks like a young Robert Mitchum.

"Yeah." His tone is clipped and when his eyes move over my shoulder, I know he's assuming something he shouldn't about the man behind me.

"This is Reid, my sister's ex-boyfriend." Introducing him as such may not be necessary—I can already tell this date with Christopher won't be going anywhere—but it's a reminder I'm in desperate need of. Especially when the heat at my back as Reid reaches around me to shake Christopher's hand sends a spark of electricity up my spine.

"Nice to meet you." Reid's breath skims across my cheek as he shakes Christopher's hand, and I hate the way my body reacts to the feel, goose bumps popping along my skin.

Afraid I won't be able to keep my reaction off my face, my gaze falls away from Christopher's, but I don't make it further than their clasped hands. The matching white knuckles have me questioning what the hell is happening.

"There you are," a voice calls from a few feet down the street, and when I glance up I can't help the small gasp that escapes.

I'm no prude. I understand wanting to feel sexy and unattainable but it's also February in the mid-Atlantic. This part of the country may have twelve seasons with a random heatwave in the middle of winter, but today is not one of those days.

It's below freezing out here and the woman now pressing herself up against Reid is dressed like it's the middle of summer—well, almost. She does have a winter coat, but just like her dress, it barely covers her ass. It's clear from the way she doesn't pull away from Reid when she turns to look at me that she's staking her claim, and I'd like to say the way she looks me up and down doesn't impact me—but it does.

I'm immediately second-guessing my outfit choice. Until seeing this woman, I thought I'd done a good job of balancing comfort with style. Driving into the heart of Gettysburg meant parking and walking to the restaurant, so I'd gone with pants to keep me warm. They're skin tight and paired with thigh high boots helping to give the illusion of long legs—which my five-foot-three frame can use all the help—but all of a sudden, I wish I'd gone with the dress I had picked as backup. Of course, the plunging neckline of the velvet shirt I'm wearing—hidden by my wool coat—is the pièce de résistance to the whole outfit.

When I got dressed this evening, I felt good in my clothes. I felt confident, like no matter what this evening brought it would be good for me, but the little smirk on this woman's lips and the heat in my date's eyes have me second-guessing all of that.

"Taylor," Reid mutters, pushing her away from him. He's not rough with his movements, but the tension in his shoulders tell me he may be a little uncomfortable with her plastered to his side. Strange, given his playboy tendencies. I thought it would be a dream come true having an attractive woman throw herself at a man like him.

Seeming to be completely ignorant of the discomfort she's causing, Taylor turns more fully to face Christopher and me while pressing her back to Reid's front.

"Who do we have here?" her shrill voice calls.

"This is Sadie and her date Christopher."

Almost instantly, Christopher juts his hand out, and when Taylor places her hand in his—in one of the most cliché moves I've ever seen—he bends, bringing the back of her hand to his lips and presses a kiss there. My eyes lift to meet Reid's and I know the shock I see there is mirrored on my own face.

What the hell? he mouths.

I shift uncomfortably, questioning everything about my decision to come on this date. What made me think it was necessary to have a date this Valentine's Day?

As if breaking out of a daze, Christopher releases Taylor's hand and turns to me, shock evident on his own face—almost like he can't believe he did that in front of me.

"Sorry," he mutters quietly, his gaze bouncing around all of us before coming back to me. "Are you ready to go in?" His voice is quiet, as if meant only for me, and with the frown marring his face, I can't stop myself from finding excuses for his lapse in judgment a moment before.

On the outside looking in, I'm sure my conversation with Reid looked like something entirely different from what it truly was. We were standing close, my back was toward Christopher, and that smirk Reid was wearing definitely looked flirty. It's not a stretch to think he might have wanted me to feel a little jealous by greeting someone else in such an effusive manner.

Or it's as simple as both of us knowing this date isn't going anywhere.

"Sure." I offer Christopher a small smile before turning for the restaurant. The four of us entering together.

CHAPTER FOUR

IT WOULD BE MY luck. My first date since the new year, and not only am I on a blind date with a woman so outside of my norm it's honestly comical Gage thought this was a good idea, but I'm sitting right next to the woman I haven't been able to stop thinking about—the one woman I should be able to forget better than anyone else.

Unable to help myself, I pull my phone from my pocket and shoot off a text.

Reid: Where in the world did you find this woman?

I'm more than surprised when I get a response.

Gage: What's wrong with Taylor?
Reid: I'm honestly struggling to see why you thought she and I would be a good fit.

It may have been rude of me to covertly text my friend during a date, but given the fact my date has spent the last ten minutes speaking exclusively to Sadie's date, I don't think she'll mind—or even notice.

Gage: All right. If I'm being honest, I didn't set you up with Taylor.

Gage: Willow heard you were looking for a date for Valentine's Day and thought her granddaughter and you would get along great...

Reid: You mean the older woman who calls the station at least once a week about the squirrel trying to steal from her?

When the three little dots appear and disappear a few times, I can't stop the soft chuckle from leaving my lips.

Gage knows he messed up.

Gage: We all know Willow makes that call every week because she's lonely in that big house by herself.

Reid: Gage. Seriously, man? Even you have said no to going on a date with her granddaughter.

Gage: Not Taylor! That was her other granddaughter!

Reid: You are so lucky you have Ava in your life now.

Reid: I would so find a way to get back at you for this if it weren't for her.

Gage: How bad can it be?

Reid: Well, I'm currently texting you instead of talking to my date, so...

Gage: Well, I mean...I'm madly in love with the woman I'm with and still texting you so...

Reid: Good point. Why are you texting me?

Gage: Ava just got in the bath and I was making her a cup of tea.

Gage: I'm off to join her, so you're on your own now.

And just like that, I know he won't be responding to another message—not that I blame him. If I had someone like

Ava in my life, I wouldn't waste my time texting me either.

The sound of the seat shifting next to me has me shoving my phone back in my pocket and lifting my head. I don't have to talk to Sadie to know she's just as irritated with her date as I am with mine.

It's not surprising my date is going the way it is considering the waiter sat Taylor, Sadie, Christopher, and me all at the same time. And instead of letting me go down the same side as Christopher when the waiter directed us to split before heading down to the center of the long table, Taylor followed him down, taking the seat next to him and almost immediately scooting closer.

Whoever decided communal dining was a good idea has never been in the uncomfortable situation I now find myself in. On one hand, I'm on a first date with a woman who hasn't even spoken ten words to me, preferring to talk to the man seated beside her like he's the only man left on earth. And on the other hand, I'm seated next to Sadie Winslow, a woman who may actually be on a first date as well. Not just a first date, but a blind date, too.

"That was a long bathroom break."

Could I have come up with something better to say to Sadie? Absolutely.

Is my brain functioning correctly? No. Not even a little bit.

But I don't think anyone can blame me. Not only have I been unable to stop thinking about the woman next to me since I saw her more than a month ago, but the second she slipped her coat off I was stunned speechless.

I saw the way Sadie's entire being tightened with tension at Taylor's appearance outside, but there's no competition between the two women. Sadie's beauty doesn't just come from her looks; it also comes from the way she carries herself. She's confident without being egotistical or brash, and I can't help but find that attractive.

Granted, I'm not going to lie and say she isn't also breathtaking with the outfit she revealed earlier. I had a hard time keeping my eyes off of her on New Year's, and now I'm desperately wishing she was seated across from me so I had a better excuse for being unable to peel my eyes away from her.

"I lied," Sadie murmurs, her voice bringing me back to the restaurant around us. "I was yelling at Madison, not in the bathroom."

"Your friend who works at the inn?" I ask, recognizing the name but struggling to picture the face to go with it.

"Yeah. She's the one who set me up on this date in the first place."

At that news I let my eyes linger on her profile, my gaze focused on the light freckles peppered across her cheek. "Set you up?"

Looking at her now, I don't miss the slight wince, as if she didn't mean to give away that piece of information, but I have no idea why it was a secret to start with.

"Yeah." She sighs, her shoulders falling for a moment before she shifts in her seat, angling her body toward me. "I was talking to Madison on the phone outside. She was talking me down from walking away once I saw the restaurant."

"Not a fan of communal dining either?" I ask, turning to face her directly.

There's no point in pretending this date with Taylor is anything more than two people dining in the same restaurant. Since the waiter walked away after dropping off our drinks she hasn't even looked at me once. I don't think Christopher even heard Sadie when she said she was going to the bathroom.

"I don't know." She shrugs, her gaze bouncing around the restaurant for a second before coming back to me. "It might be fun on some other date, but not a first date. I mean, the nerves are already high enough, why add the pressure of dealing with strangers sitting right next to you? Overhearing every word said? No, thank you."

"I can't say I disagree with you."

"How did you end up here?" Sadie settles farther into her chair, leaning her elbow on the back of her seat. The way she's twisted her torso causes her shirt to shift, exposing just a tiny bit more skin and it takes effort for me to keep my eyes on hers.

"You remember Gage?"

Sadie and I may not have spent a ton of time around each other in the past, but there were a few gatherings Summer and I held in both Ashford Falls and Stonebridge Hollow where Gage and Sadie both would have been in attendance.

"Kind of. You work with him at the station, right?"

"Correct. Anyway, he's the one who set all this up. Though, apparently, *he* didn't actually set any of it up and just went along with what someone else said."

She looks at me in confusion but before either of us can say anything else, the waiter returns and it's clear from the pinched look on his face, he doesn't understand what's going on with our tables.

"Sorry." I offer an apologetic smile to the waiter before trying to get Taylor's attention. On the second attempt, I decide maybe it's not worth it. "Can you give us a few more minutes?" I ask the waiter.

"Of course." It's a pitying look he throws our way before he walks off, but I'm honestly fine with how this night is turning out.

I never thought I'd end up in this situation, but I'm not mad at this opportunity to spend time with the woman I can't stop thinking about.

"You want to get out of here?" I turn back to Sadie and almost laugh at the look of pure relief that passes over her face at the idea as she nods her head emphatically. "Let's go."

The sight of me standing finally grabs Taylor's attention. "Where are you going?"

"Look…" I smile, trying to make sure they know I mean no hard feelings. "Clearly, the two of you have some connection that we don't, so we're gonna let you both explore that and get out of here."

"No," Christopher says, standing from his own seat and reaching for Sadie.

"It's really okay. You two have a good evening, this place just isn't my vibe." I'm not sure how true that is, but I like that she doesn't make a scene out of what's happening.

Christopher looks like he's thinking about putting up a fight, but after I drop a couple twenties on the table and begin helping Sadie into her coat, he simply nods and sits back down. Sadie and I offer one more parting smile to both Taylor and Christopher before we lose sight of them as we walk out the door.

"Is it sad that this wasn't my worst first date?" Sadie asks when we make it back onto the street.

"I honestly don't know." I chuckle, resting my hand on the small of her back and guiding her gently to the side. "This was pretty bad. Not even twenty minutes into the date and you're walking out, with another guy no less."

"Oh, the horror stories I could share." She smiles, tilting her head back to meet my eyes. Even in her heels, I still tower over her.

I've never noticed it before, and I'm suddenly wondering if I was oblivious to it or if she's never truly smiled in my presence, but the dimple in her right cheek captures my attention. I desperately want to touch it—with my finger, my lips, my tongue—I'm not picky.

I swear there's a moment where Sadie leans toward me, as if she's drawn to me the same way I am to her, but the sound of a horn shakes both of us from whatever moment we were having.

"Well." Sadie steps back, clearing her throat. "I guess I can't be too mad I ran into you tonight, but I won't lie. I'm hoping it doesn't happen again." I open my mouth to argue that fact, but before I can, she turns and walks away. "Have a nice life, asshole," she shouts over her shoulder.

I wonder if she still thinks I'm an asshole or it's a way to remind herself she's supposed to hate me.

MARCH

CHAPTER FIVE

Sadie

"CHUG IT, SADIE!" WYATT shouts from one side of me, while his sister laughs on the other.

I can't, for the life of me, figure out why I agreed to come out with Madison and her brother, but I won't lie—I'm having a great time. Maybe Madison was right, and this is exactly what I needed. She may have gotten that date horribly wrong on Valentine's day, but barhopping in Baltimore for St. Patrick's Day is far more fun than I thought it would be.

I laugh as I slam the empty pint glass onto the bar, the shot glass rattling around inside of it. My arms fly into the air to show I'm done. I know there's not a chance in hell I finished before everyone else, but I still had a blast competing in the chugging contest.

"Way to let go, babe." Madison wraps her arm around my waist pulling me into her side making me stumble.

"All right. I think I need to slow down. Maybe a few glasses of water before anything else to drink." I lean against the bar, trying to get one of the bartenders' attention.

"That's no fun." Madison pouts. "That's why we brought Wyatt with us, to keep us safe."

The side-eye I throw her way tells her exactly what I think

of that. Wyatt may have been by my side less than a minute ago, but glancing over my shoulder, he's now in the middle of the bar hitting on a woman who's been making eyes at him for the last hour.

"I love you and your brother, but we both know he was never going to be our DD tonight."

I was shocked when Madison told me Wyatt would be the one joining us for the bar crawl and not her boyfriend, but considering Wyatt's rarely home these days, it didn't surprise me he offered to tag along. Not only so he could keep his little sister safe, but so he could spend time with her when he had so little to give.

"Well, duh," she rolls her eyes. "That's why we Ubered here."

I don't even try to hold in the laugh. "I know. I just meant, none of us were going to be the sober one tonight, so we're all responsible for keeping ourselves safe. Besides, it's not safety I'm worried about. It's how I'm going to feel in the morning if I don't stay hydrated tonight."

"Boo!" she practically shouts, making both of us laugh. "Stop being such an adult! We aren't that old yet."

She's not wrong; being twenty-eight I've still got lots of life to live, but being hungover at twenty-eight is very different than being hungover at twenty-one.

"Speak for yourself." I laugh.

I know she's upset and looking to get a little wild in an effort to forget her boyfriend bailed on us—on her—today, and while I'll support her however I can, I'm not in the mood to battle a massive hangover tomorrow.

Before Madison has a chance to remind me I'm only a year older than her, one of the bartenders comes back this way. "What can I get you, babe?"

"Just a water, please." I know the smile I offer is tight, but the combination of the nickname and the flirtatious look that feels far more creepy than anything else has me more than ready to move on to a new bar.

One glance at Wyatt over my shoulder and I know we aren't going anywhere. Madison follows my gaze and moves toward him, determination in her eyes. I have no idea why she's upset with him; I knew this is exactly what Wyatt would be up to today when he agreed to come out with us.

"Here you go." My attention is brought back to the bartender as he places the plastic cup on the bar.

Without thinking anything of it, I reach for it quickly, only now realizing just how thirsty I am. Before the cup is even lifted off the bar, a hand closes around my wrist, pulling me close and forcing me to my toes, the bar digging into my ribs.

My grip on the cup immediately loosens and my eyes rise to the man in shock. *What the fuck?*

"My shift ends in thirty."

"Are you kidding?" I ask in disbelief. "In what world is this how you ask someone…to what? Stick around?" I twist my wrist, trying to break free from his grip, but his hold only tightens and my heart rate spikes. "Let go of me."

The bartender doesn't have a chance to respond before a hand lands on his forearm, a smooth voice washing over both of us. "I think the lady was very clear. She's not interested."

My gaze roams from the white knuckled grip on the bartender's arm, up the corded forearm of my rescuer, to the handsome face of a stranger. My shock and racing heartbeat are for an entirely different reason now—a much more pleasant reason.

"Oh my god, Sadie!" Madison shouts back at my side. "Are you okay?"

The hold on my wrist disappears, and I swear I hear a grunt from the bartender, but all of my focus is forced back to Madison, who now has Wyatt behind her, worry etched across both their brows.

"I'm fine…" My words trail off as my gaze shifts to the man beside me, hoping he'll jump in to introduce himself.

The smirk that grows across his lips, causing a dimple to pop in both cheeks makes me melt a little on the spot. "Just a handsy bartender who doesn't know how to take no for an answer."

"Thanks for stepping in," Wyatt murmurs, his eyes moving from mine to the man before he sticks his hand out. "I should've been paying closer attention."

Without really thinking about my actions, I slap Wyatt's hand away, glaring at him. "That's really not your job, *friend*." I emphasize the word, desperately wanting to make it clear there is nothing between Wyatt and me.

For the first time since New Year's, my reaction to an attractive man is exactly what I want—and probably—need it to be. If this man is single, and interested in me, I need him to know there's 100 percent a chance with me.

Madison, being the best friend a girl can ask for, immediately catches on. "Wyatt, Julie's waiting for you." She gestures in the direction they came from, pushing him back toward the woman he was hitting on only minutes before.

"You're the one who pulled me over here," he hisses, the worry morphing to annoyance at his little sister.

The two of them continue to argue as Madison discreetly maneuvers them away from the bar. The heat washing all over me has nothing to do with the attractive man next to me and everything to do with my embarrassment.

"Sorry about that." I slowly turn back to my hero, hoping

the blush I know is evident on my cheeks isn't noticeable in the low lighting of the bar. "Thanks for helping me out." I gesture to the bar at my side, the space the bartender occupied now void of anyone.

"It's no problem. I'm sure you had it handled, but that doesn't mean you should have to deal with assholes."

Swoon. Why is that so sexy? A man knowing a woman can handle herself, but still stepping in to support her?

"I won't lie. I was a little nervous. His grip just kept getting tighter and tighter." I lift my hands between us, my left hand gently gripping my right wrist, but then a bigger hand pulls my hands apart, his fingers smoothing over my arm as he studies the red marks clearly visible.

"I'd be a little concerned if you weren't nervous." His words are soft, barely loud enough to be heard over the crowd and music around us. "Does it hurt?" he asks, his finger probing around my wrist.

"Not really," I breathe out, unable to look away from the man in front of me. His gaze is entirely focused on my arm held gently in his, but I'm still completely entranced by him.

He's tall—but then most people are when you're only five foot, three inches—and well-built. A man who clearly takes great pride in his appearance. His light hair is styled back from his face, and his high cheek bones and angular jaw are on full display from my angle. The man is the definition of good looking.

"I don't think anything serious is wrong with it, but you should keep an eye on it."

"Yeah. Okay," I whisper.

His gaze lifts to mine, a small smile growing on his lips. "You all right?"

I mentally slap myself at the ridiculousness of how I'm

acting. Clearing my throat, I gently pull my hand back from his grip before responding. "Yeah, I'm good."

He studies me a moment before nodding his head and standing back to his full height. "Good, then can I buy you a drink?"

I tuck a piece of hair behind my ear, a smile of my own growing. "I don't let strangers buy me drinks."

"That sounds like a good rule." He lifts his hand between us. "I'm Kyle."

"Nice to meet you, Kyle. I'm Sadie." I place my hand in his, the smooth feel of his hand sending a spark up my arm.

- - - - -

WHAT'S HAPPENING? WHY IS *everything spinning around me?*

I try to pull away from the person behind me, but the grip on my hips tightens. "Where are you going?" a deep voice whispers in my ear.

Do I know you?

"I don't feel good. I think I'm going to be sick." I try to pull away again, but stumble, falling back into the body behind me.

"It's okay. I've got you."

"No." I spin, pushing at the hard chest. "I don't want you."

I try to focus on the face before me, but I can't. Everything around me shifts and blurs. The hands around me are torn away and I feel myself falling, but before I hit the ground, something catches me.

"Sadie?" a familiar voice calls, but it's like everything around me fades away.

I can't see anything.

"I'm scared," I whisper, tears slipping down my cheeks.

"I know. But it's okay now. Everything's going to be okay."

I feel a light touch brush hair off my face before everything becomes weightless and I stop hearing anything.

CHAPTER SIX

Reid

I FEEL LIKE A stalker.

It was one thing keeping an eye on her when I saw her at the first bar, The Rusty Anchor. And it might not have been a big deal convincing Ava and Gage to move onto another bar when I saw her leaving the first time. But the second and third time? I can't find any legitimate reason for that.

"All right. What in the world is going on with you?" Ava asks when it's just the two of us.

"What do you mean?" I feign ignorance, my gaze trained on the woman I still haven't gotten off my mind.

I know I'm not fooling either of them, especially after that last bar, but even if I hadn't literally pushed both of them out the door, they were already on to me. Ava and Gage are both incredibly smart people all on their own, but add in their occupations—a lawyer and a cop—and there's no way I'll ever pull one over on them.

"Want to try that again?"

My focus shifts from the redhead across the bar to the brunette before me. I'm honestly a little surprised it took her this long to ask. I was pretty sure she caught onto something after The Rusty Anchor. My request to move on was too abrupt, even for me.

"There's a woman."

"Of course there is." Ava's eyes twinkle, a teasing glint shining through.

"I know it sounds cliché, but not like that."

Her smile slips, and I'm not sure if it's because of my tone or the fact that my eyes can't stay focused on her for more than a few seconds at a time. "That definitely sounds cliché, but I believe you. What's up?"

"Long story short?" I wait for her nod before continuing. "I'm apparently obsessed with my ex-girlfriend's younger sister."

"Sorry." Ava lifts her hand, as if asking me to pause. "I know there's more coming, but I'm confused by the apparently part of that statement. How is it 'apparently'?" she asks, putting air quotes around the word.

"I don't know!" I practically shout, my agitation at the situation getting the best of me.

"Whoa, don't yell at my girlfriend," Gage's stern voice comes from behind me.

I didn't need the words. My head falls forward and my hands rise in defeat. "That was in no way directed at Ava, but I'm still sorry for my tone."

"You're fine." Ava reaches for me, bringing my attention back to her. "I think you need to start at the beginning and tell the long story." Her voice is gentle, compassion pouring off her in waves.

My gaze shifts back to Sadie. I need to confirm that she's still okay.

Part of me wants to say the only reason I've been following her all night is because I saw her best friend leave The Rusty Anchor without her, but I'm pretty sure I would have followed her no matter what.

If I hadn't been watching Sadie like a hawk, I might have been surprised when Madison left. I don't know her well, but Madison doesn't seem like the kind of person to leave her best friend in a bar over an hour from their hometown.

It was clear Madison was in distress, and after a very lengthy conversation, one that had both of them pulling their phones out and messing with some setting, Madison was out the door and Sadie was back in the arms of some douchebag.

When I walked into that first bar and saw her cozied up with the guy, I seriously thought about turning around and leaving, but something in my gut told me not to. My gut and I still aren't on the best terms, but I'm trying like hell to trust it. Though, tonight is definitely testing my resolve.

There's no apparently about it. I am 100 percent obsessed with Sadie, and I'm not entirely sure I want to fight it. Not that I think she wants anything to do with me.

Just as I'm about to bring my focus back to Ava and Gage, Sadie shifts, pushing at the man behind her. I don't wait to see what else happens, I'm moving toward them as quickly as the crowd around me will allow.

"No. I don't want you." Her words are slurred and everything about her indicates she's not okay. She can barely keep her eyes open as her head bounces around like she can't hold it up any more and her feet tangle together like she doesn't have control of them.

"Get your hands off her," I seethe, yanking the blond away from her. I don't hesitate to reach for Sadie, catching her before she falls. "Sadie?"

Her eyes are closed and I fear she's passed out.

"I'm scared," she whispers, tears slipping down both her cheeks.

"I know." Relief courses through me hearing her voice, no matter how soft it is. "But it's okay now. Everything's going to be okay."

Gently, I brush her sweat-soaked hair away from her face, seeing a quick glimpse of her hazel eyes when they flutter open, only for her entire body to sag against me a moment later.

"Sadie?" I shake her gently, and when she doesn't even twitch I start to panic. I give myself one breath and then focus.

Checking her pulse and feeling the steady beat releases the vestiges of fear coursing through me.

"Reid?" Ava's voice breaks through my fog, pulling me back to the bar around us. "Oh my god! Sadie," she gasps.

I don't know how they know each other, but now isn't the time to figure it out. With Ava's help, I get Sadie lifted into my arms, one arm under her knees and the other around her back, holding her close.

"I don't know who the fuck you are, but you're done here." Gage's authoritative voice sounds from behind me, and I know without looking he's talking to the asshole who did this.

"Don't let him go," I boom. "We won't know until we get her to the hospital, but I'd bet my badge he drugged her."

"Whoa, man. I don't know what you're talking about. I just met her." He lifts his hands, a look of practiced innocence crossing his features.

"Yeah, no." Gage chuckles, but the sound is dark. "Today's not your lucky day, man."

"What's the problem here?" A man with *SECURITY* stamped across his shirt pushes through the crowd, his eyes immediately moving to the woman in my arms.

"He slipped something in her drink," I say, using my head to gesture to the asshole.

"He's insane. I didn't do anything. I was just dancing with her when she started complaining about not feeling well. Then this jackass showed up spouting this nonsense."

"Here's what's going to happen." Ava steps forward, bringing everyone's attention to her. "You're taking Sadie to the hospital. Gage and I will meet you there," she says, her tone holding no room for argument. At my nod she switches her focus to the guy from security. "You're going to call the cops and report that you're holding an individual on a charge of suspected assault."

"Who the hell—"

"I'd shut your mouth if I were you." Gage doesn't need to raise his voice; it's clear he's not taking this guy's crap.

"All right," the security guard shouts, garnering the attention of everyone around us. "The cops and an ambulance have been called. Let's get her"—the man gestures to Sadie—"to the back room, away from the crowd. And you"—he gestures to the blond asshole as another guy from security shows up—"are going with him. No arguments."

With security involved, there's nothing else I can do about the man who did this, so I put all my attention to the woman in my arms and follow the security guard. The crowd separates like the Red Sea, letting us pass without issue.

"You're okay," I whisper to Sadie, even though I know she can't hear me. "I've got you."

"You know her?" the security guard asks as he opens a door to what looks like the manager's office.

I step into the space, Ava and Gage not far behind me. "Yeah, she's a friend."

Sadie might not agree to that label now, but if I have

anything to say about it, hopefully she will soon.

"All right. I'll leave you in here and bring the paramedics back when they get here." He offers a slight nod before closing the door softly behind him.

I move toward the couch in the room, gently lying Sadie down. A soft groan leaves her lips and I find myself kneeling beside her, brushing hair from her face. Peaceful is the only word I can think of for how she looks and yet I know it's not what she is right now. She might be unconscious and technically unaware of what's going on around her, but her last words were of fear.

"Is this who we've been following?" Ava's gentle voice sounds from beside me before I feel her kneel next to me.

"Yeah," I murmur, slipping Sadie's right hand into my left and cupping her cheek in the palm of my other hand. I can't take my eyes off her, and—if I'm honest—I don't want to.

All of a sudden, I'm incredibly grateful I listened to my gut.

Did I assume my dick was guiding my gut when I convinced Ava and Gage to leave The Rusty Anchor? Absolutely, I did. And my dick may have played a big part in it, but something about that guy didn't feel right.

"She's your ex's younger sister?" Ava's voice brings me back to the present.

"Yes." I know Ava's looking for more, but I can't focus on that right now. All of my focus is on a woman I shouldn't be focusing on at all—at least not in the way I've been obsessing over her since New Year's.

"How do you know her?" Gage asks Ava.

It's a question I want the answer to, just not one I'm capable of vocalizing right now.

"We went to college together. We met at the library one

night my third year and just clicked."

I had no idea Ava and Sadie went to the same school, but it doesn't surprise me that they found each other. Ava and Sadie have the kind of personality you can't help but be drawn to. I'd be more surprised to hear they existed in the same space and *didn't* find each other.

Before Ava can share anything else, the door to the office opens. The same security guard who escorted us to the office is there with two paramedics and a police officer. Without waiting to be told, I stand from my place at Sadie's side and step back, facing the officer to answer the questions I know he has.

It takes effort not to follow the paramedics out the door once they get Sadie on the gurney. I might want to be with her when she wakes up, but there's a good chance I'm the last person she'll want to see.

I grab Gage's arm, stopping him before he's able to walk out the door after Ava. "Maybe don't tell Sadie I'm the one who helped her tonight," I tell him softly.

"What? Why?"

I've come to accept I was wrong about Sadie. She's nothing like her sister and would never treat others the way Summer has. And because Sadie is nothing like her sister, she'll never allow herself to betray her. No matter what happens.

"It's not important." I shake my head, my gaze moving to the door where Ava appears, her eyebrows pinched in question. "Can you keep me updated, though?"

I see the question in Gage's eyes, but he doesn't ask. He simply nods, placing his hand on my shoulder and squeezes once before he moves toward Ava.

No matter what, Sadie's in good hands now.

MAY

CHAPTER SEVEN

✦

Sadie

"ARE YOU SURE THERE'S nothing I can help you with?" I ask Ava from across the kitchen island.

"No! I want you to sit and talk with me."

Two and a half months since Ava and I reconnected, and she's still giving me that look of worry. Don't get me wrong, I completely understand where the worry comes from, but it's been *two and a half months*. It was a terrifying situation, and it's definitely made me stick close to home and question the intentions of everyone around me, but in the grand scheme of things, I'm okay.

Nothing truly horrible happened to me, not like so many other women around the world. I was lucky, Gage and Ava appeared at exactly the moment I needed them most.

Did it change my life?

Yes. Just not in the way Kyle most likely intended.

"Ava." I sigh. "I'm fine. Please stop looking at me like I'm going to break. I'm stronger than I look."

"No, Sadie." Ava's eyes fall closed for a second before they open again and she's moving around the island to take both my hands in hers. "I swear to you, I know how strong you are. Whatever look you think you're seeing has absolutely nothing to do with you." Her grip on my hands tightens as her eyes fall away from mine. When she lifts her gaze back to me, tears well in the corners.

"Ava," I whisper.

"I'm just glad you're all right," she interrupts before I can say anything else, pulling me into a fierce hug.

I let Ava hug me as long as she needs, only pulling away when her arms loosen from around me. I know what happened to me that night brings back bad memories for her, and while I hate that we're both part of this messed-up club, I'm incredibly grateful to have her in my corner.

My experience and hers are different. I know she'd say neither is better or worse than the other, but I don't agree. Kyle never had the chance to lay a hand on me, and while Gage might have saved Ava before anything went too far, Ava can't say the same about what happened to her.

But no matter how we view our experiences, she's been my rock through this whole thing. Standing by my side, guiding me through the legal side of everything.

I don't need a lawyer to represent me or anything, but it's nice having someone with me who understands all the legal jargon the district attorney throws my way.

It's insane to me, the fact that I went through a traumatic experience, and to get justice I have to experience the whole thing over and over again. Not just reliving the feelings and events from that night, but also preparing for every aspect of my life to be put under a microscope and for them to question how sure I am Kyle had anything to do with what happened to me, since I can't remember most of that night.

To an extent, I understand the recounting of everything that happened, but that doesn't make it easier. And no matter what, I'll never understand how a person's past can determine the validity of the violation I experienced. How I may or may not have lived my life doesn't lessen the fact that I was drugged and someone planned to take advantage of my inebriated state.

No means no. Regardless of how many men I have or have not slept with.

And a person as unaware of their surroundings as I was definitely couldn't have given consent to anything.

Before either of us can say anything else, Gage's voice calls from the front of the house. "Honey, I'm home and I come bearing drinks and ice."

"We're in the kitchen, but coolers are ready for you out back," Ava responds, wiping under her eyes before moving back to the other side of the kitchen island.

"Thanks, Rebel," he hollers, before his words become quieter as he heads back outside.

"Is he talking to himself?" I ask, moving to wash my hands so I can help Ava with the rest of the prep.

"He could be, but I think he said one of the guys was coming early to help him set up." Ava passes me a cutting board and knife, gesturing to the celery beside me, finally letting me help.

"Is this one of the guys from his unit?" I ask, curious who Ava means.

I'm still getting to know Gage, but I know he served in the Army for twelve years, and he'd still be serving if it hadn't been for an accident that put him behind a desk.

Being here for Memorial Day makes the holiday more real for me than ever before. Knowing someone who served in the armed forces, someone who lost the people we're supposed to be honoring, hits far closer to home than I realized it would.

Waking up in the hospital with a man I kind of recognized

but didn't really know next to me was truly terrifying, especially when I had no recollection of anything that happened after walking into that last bar. But Gage's calm demeanor as he quietly explained he was a friend of a friend, sitting with me until they got back from the bathroom somehow made it a little better.

I was still confused and scared, but there was something about him that told me I was safe—that nothing could hurt me. Of course, learning more about him from Ava, about his history in the military and his current occupation, helped me understand how his presence brought me a sense of peace.

As I started to relax and remember who Gage was, I was shocked to learn the friend Gage referred to was Ava—someone I hadn't seen or spoken to in years—and not Reid.

The last I heard, Ava was working in Boston. But I recognized her the moment I saw her, and seeing her calmed me even more. Not that the fear of waking up in the hospital wasn't still reeling inside me.

While learning I'd been drugged had drastically changed how I viewed the world, in some twisted way, I was glad it brought Ava back into my life. We'd been texting each other almost daily since that night and she'd come out to Stonebridge Hollow a few times.

When Ava invited me to Gage's Memorial Day barbeque, I knew I couldn't say no. Both of them were there for me when I needed a friendly face most, and being here on a day I knew couldn't be the easiest for Gage seemed like a small way to repay them for their friendship.

"No. None of them are making it this year. It's just his family and friends from town," Ava says a little distractedly.

Before I can ask her for clarification on who "one of the guys is," the back door opens and Gage's laugh precedes his entrance, another laugh joining him.

"Sadie, you're here!" Gage yells when he sees me. He doesn't hesitate to come around the kitchen and pull me into a quick hug.

I haven't known him long, but one thing I've learned is that Gage Flynn is a massive teddy bear when it comes to the people he loves. And while we may have only *really* known each other for a little over two months, Gage is quickly becoming the big brother I always wish I had, and I know he's starting to look at me like one of his numerous siblings.

The man has one complicated family tree, but it also makes him one of the most caring people I've ever met, and I couldn't be happier he's part of Ava's life.

As quickly as he enters my space, he moves out of it and over to Ava, pulling her in for a very different kind of embrace, one of so much love I feel a pinch in my chest.

I'm genuinely happy for both of them. The love they so clearly share is one for the ages, and seeing it first-hand makes me wish I had it myself.

Though, if anyone deserves the happiness they've found, it's the two of them. Even if we didn't have time to catch up since St. Patrick's Day, I would have said the same thing—at least about Ava. These past two months aren't the only time I've leaned heavily on her friendship.

"Sadie Winslow, as I live and breathe." Reid's voice pulls my attention his way, and while there's a smirk stretched across his lips, I immediately notice how fake it is. His eyes don't shine with mischief and the laugh lines in the corners are nowhere in sight. "If you wanted to see me, all you had to do was ask. No reason to stalk me."

The concern I felt growing disappears as quickly as it started and I roll my eyes. "Can you really call it stalking if I was here first?"

"Hmm," he hums. "All right, stalking may not be the right word, but it is shocking to find you standing in my friend's kitchen. I didn't know you knew Gage outside of those few encounters you had more than three years ago when Summer and I were dating."

I squint my eyes at him, trying to decide if I care enough to explain my connection.

Reid Alexander means nothing to me. For one thing, he *can't* mean anything to me—he's my sister's ex. But beyond that, he's a jerk. The stories my sister told about him were enough for me to recognize that, but add in the snide comments he made at New Year's and on Valentine's Day, and that's proof of what Summer said about him.

"I know Ava." I sigh. If I'm planning on continuing this friendship with Ava—which I very much want—then I might have to get used to seeing Reid more, which means finding a way to be civil with one another. "We went to college together."

Reid's brows lift in surprise. "Didn't Ava go to Harvard?"

"Yes," I hiss, hearing the disbelieving tone in his voice.

I open my mouth to give Reid a piece of my mind—what right does he have to sound so disbelieving at the thought I went to Harvard?

But before I can, Gage slaps him on the back, dragging him out the back door.

If I'm being honest, when I walked away from him after our dates from hell on Valentine's Day, I had to remind myself I'm not supposed to like him. I kind of thought we might be turning a corner in whatever this thing was between us, but four months later and we're right back to where we started the year.

It's better that way, I know it is, but that doesn't stop that pinch from returning when I see him laugh with Gage out the back window.

CHAPTER EIGHT

Reid

SEEING SADIE DOES SOMETHING to me. The pinch in my chest at the sight of her isn't new, but it is different today.

Gage—being the loyal man he is—kept his word. He didn't only keep me up to date while she was in the hospital, he also made sure I knew what was going on with her emotionally too. I didn't need the updates about her legal case, but he made sure I stayed up to date on that as well.

I knew showing up today I'd run into Sadie and I thought I was ready for it, but clearly I wasn't.

She called me an asshole the last two times we spoke, and I couldn't blame her if she called me an asshole today. I may not have actually said the words, but my tone definitely implied I was shocked she got into Harvard. I don't even know where that tone came from.

That's not true. I may have known Sadie went to Harvard, but what reason would I have to remember that information over the last three years?

Summer rarely talked about anyone in her family, so Sadie was never the main focus of any conversation. Honestly, I only remember Summer talking about her when there was some planned activity she knew Sadie would be at too.

Which, in hindsight, probably should have been something I paid attention to far earlier in our relationship. Maybe if I had I wouldn't have been so blindsided by the person she showed herself to be.

Either way, Sadie going to Harvard was one of the few things I knew about her from my time dating her sister. It was a point of contention for Summer, that her younger sister had accomplished something so prestigious—something her parents loved to brag about. Yet another moment I should have seen the person Summer truly was.

My brother and I aren't close, and I don't have the best of relationship with my parents, but had Bryce made it into some fancy school, my parents wouldn't have been the only people bragging about that accomplishment.

Learning that she and Ava knew each other because they went to the same school wasn't the shocking piece of information that night. I simply never imagined them running into each other since there are a few years between them and they had two entirely different majors.

"You okay, man?" Gage's voice pulls me back to the moment, forcing my gaze away from the woman across the yard from me—the woman I've been struggling to keep my eyes off of all afternoon.

"Yeah, just lost in thought." I shake my head, trying to focus on the conversation before me. "What were you saying?"

"Nothing important." Gage waves me off. "What were you looking at?"

"Not what, who." Declan smirks, his eyes on the same group of women mine were just on. I'm sure his attention is on the woman with the camera in her hand, but my redhead is over there with her.

"Ah. I don't even need to look." Gage laughs, loving the place I've found myself.

It wasn't long ago I was giving him a hard time about how obsessed he was with Ava—and still is, if we're all honest with ourselves. But he laughed it off and told me I'd understand when I found *my* person. While I didn't disagree with him on the entire concept of always thinking about and wanting to be with the person you know in your soul is meant for you, I did disagree with the idea I'd ever find that person for myself.

Maybe it was a simple fact of never meeting the right person, but I met Sadie Winslow six years ago. If she was the person my soul called to, wouldn't we have felt that spark instantly?

Granted, I did feel something I'd never felt before when I saw her on New Year's Eve. Something that one could easily describe as being obsessed.

Not that I can be obsessed with Sadie Winslow.

"The redhead, right?" Gage asks, sticking true to his word and not looking behind him.

"Oh yeah." Declan chuckles.

"Okay. This really isn't necessary," I almost plead.

"It most definitely is. Do you remember all the teasing you did when Ava and I first started seeing each other? All the teasing you still do?"

"You and I have only really started hanging out and you've given me plenty of crap about how I am with Quinn." Declan chuckles, no real heat in his words.

"Okay, but I mean…you and Quinn haven't even known each other a year and you're getting married in a month and a half."

I know there's a lot more to Quinn and Declan's story than

meets the eye. They may have officially met last October, but they've both spent the last six years hearing about the other person from Quinn's family—her brothers and her dad. And if it weren't for Quinn's dad getting sick, it would have taken even longer for the two of them to find each other.

"What can I say? When you know, you know." Declan's eyes move back over to Quinn, and the look of pure contentment and love that passes over his face has that pinch back in my chest.

I want that feeling, and that thought shocks me. I've never wished for something so serious before. I've never wanted something so permanent and real. Not even when I was with Summer, and I was with her for three years.

"And when you know," Declan continues, bringing his focus back to Gage and me, "you don't really want to put anything on hold. You just want to dive in with both feet."

It's almost comical how the three of us turn to look at the three women across the yard from us and how Sadie, Quinn, and Ava turn to look at us as soon as Quinn catches on.

I don't doubt for a second that Gage and Declan are entirely focused on their other halves, and it's likely the smiles between the two couples completely distracts everyone but me from Sadie's glare.

I don't need to hear the word to know she's calling me an asshole in her mind right now. I can see it clear as day in her eyes, all the way from the other side of the yard.

"So, what's the story?" Declan asks, his attention back on me.

"Yeah, you haven't even filled me in on that. All I know is she's Summer's younger sister." Gage takes a gulp of his beer, his stance relaxing as if he's preparing to be here awhile.

"What else do you need to know?" I huff. "In what world

can I date Summer's younger sister?"

"Who's Summer?" Declan interrupts.

Declan isn't necessarily new to town, but he didn't grow up in Ashford Falls, and as he mentioned, the two of us didn't really start hanging out until Gage and Ava came clean about their relationship.

It was inevitable that Declan and I would become friends as Gage and him grew closer. Declan and Gage—just as Declan and I—were more like acquaintances until the truth about Gage's relationship with his sister was made public.

The only one missing from our normal group is Caleb, Quinn's older brother. But considering his wife Emily just gave birth five days ago. I'm not surprised they couldn't make it today.

"Summer is my ex-girlfriend," I answer Declan's question.

"They dated for almost three years," Gage offers when I don't say anything else.

"That's pretty serious." Declan's eyes widen in surprise.

"So serious we all thought they were going to end up married."

My gaze falls to my feet as I shuffle uncomfortably at the thought. I knew when Summer and I were together that people thought I'd propose to her, and if I'm honest, I thought I'd propose to her too. But looking back on that time in my life, I can't figure out what the fuck I was thinking.

I recognize that a large part of my feelings now come down to hindsight, but from the very start of our relationship, Summer showed me exactly how closed off she was. In reality, it was a bunch of small things, but had I been paying better attention, maybe I would have seen them for what they were. Things like never holding the door open when she saw someone only a few steps behind her. Or never saying please and thank you to our waiter when we went out to eat. Or the fact she never spoke of her family except in moments of annoyance.

Add in the way I've constantly been thinking about Sadie and haven't shown an inkling of interest in anyone else since I saw her on New Year's, and marrying Summer would have been the worst mistake I could have made.

My thoughts of Summer were never as all-consuming as my thoughts of Sadie have been. And in the grand scheme of things, I've spent a total of maybe ten hours in her presence since we ran into each other on New Year's. Obsessed may be too small of a word when it comes to Sadie Winslow.

"What happened?" Declan asks, bringing me back to the present.

"She showed her true colors," I murmur, bringing my eyes back up to his. "She wasn't a good person. She was rude and disrespectful to practically everyone around her, she thought people who liked simple things were below her. We just didn't fit."

My attention is drawn away from Declan and Gage by the sound of a full-body laugh, and when I turn to look, I'm stuck speechless. Sadie is folded in half, barely holding herself up. I can only assume something Max, Quinn's little brother, did or said caused that reaction if the proud smile stretched across his face is anything to go by. It only takes her a second to gather herself enough to pull Max into her side, giving him a lighthearted noogie in response.

If there was any lingering doubt about Sadie being anything like her sister, it disappears in that moment. Not only did Summer hate kids, but she wouldn't have been caught dead bringing so much attention to herself—at least, not for laughing in such an unsophisticated manner.

"I know that look." Gage slaps me on the back and I startle at the sudden jolt. "You're a goner, man. Not a chance in hell you make it out the other side unchanged."

"What?" I ask in confusion.

"The situation with Sadie may be complicated, I won't lie and say it isn't, but don't let complicated stop you from even trying," Gage says seriously; more serious than I've seen him this entire conversation. "The one thing I know without a shadow of a doubt? The only thing in life you'll regret is not even trying."

"And don't do her thinking for her," Declan offers. "The worst thing you can do is assume you know what she wants. Let her have a say in what she does with her life."

"Wait a second. I don't know what you think you see, but you're wrong. There's nothing going on with Sadie and me."

Gage and Declan look at each other, a silent conversation happening in the few seconds before they both turn back to me.

"Live in the land of denial all you want, but deep down, we all know you want to go there with Sadie." Gage claps his hand to my shoulder and squeezes before turning and walking away, Declan only a few paces behind him.

I watch them make their way over to their other halves and a spark of jealousy courses through my veins.

How in the world have I found myself in this situation? And what the hell am I supposed to do now?

My eyes drift to the beautiful redhead, and I don't even try to fight it anymore. Gage and Declan are right; I am a goner when it comes to Sadie. I just don't know if I'm ready to act on the truth yet.

JULY

CHAPTER NINE

"WHAT DID WE DO to deserve working the festival today?" Gage asks as we step out of the station and onto Main Street.

"The whole department is working today." I laugh.

"Yeah, but we could've had the morning shift so we'd be able to enjoy this evening," Gage grumbles.

"We both know if we weren't working we'd be at home."

"Really?" Gage asks in disbelief. "I'm not gonna lie. That surprises me. Not me being at home." His smile is tight and more forced than anything I've ever seen from him, but I understand why it's there after the week he's had.

It's been less than a week since Quinn's dad passed, and while everyone knew it was coming, it hasn't stopped the entire town from being rocked by it. Scott Marks was the kind of man most men should strive to be. He loved his family with everything he had, cared for those he held dear, wanted the best for this town, and went above and beyond in every effort to help those around him.

I know the town hurts from the loss, but for those closest

to him, I can't imagine the pain they're in.

"But *you* not going out and enjoying the festival?" He winks, bringing levity back into the moment. "That surprises me."

I open my mouth to respond, but his steps falter as he grabs my shoulder, a soft chuckle leaving his lips. "Wait. I take that back. It might have shocked me a few months ago, but after seeing you at my house for Memorial Day…" His words trail off, no need for him to spell out what he's trying to say.

Minus that blind date on Valentine's Day, I haven't been seen with another woman all year. No dates, no drinks at the bar, no one-night stands, nothing. And since the barbeque, I've spent even more time and energy obsessing over a certain someone.

Have I figured out what I want to do about these feelings? Not even a little bit.

"How are Ava, Declan, and the Markses doing?" I ask, changing the subject.

It's a low blow, using the loss of Scott as a distraction, but when it comes down to it, I'm surprised Gage is even here today.

Ava and Declan may not have been biologically related to Scott, but he was more of a father to them than theirs ever was. I know they're feeling this loss just as deeply as the kids Scott raised.

I'd have thought Gage would take the day off to be close to Ava, supporting her in whatever way she needed most.

"I'm sorry," I whisper, wanting to take back my words.

"They're all right. All things considered," Gage answers, as if my words don't hurt him. "They're all staying close to the house today." He offers a closed-mouth smile, and the look in his eyes makes me regret the question even more than I already did.

I'm such an asshole.

How ironic is it that the moment that word runs through my brain, the woman who can't stop calling me an asshole shows up on the street in front of us?

"Boy, do I love karma." The words are so quiet from Gage I'm not sure I hear him correctly, but his next words are loud enough to grab the attention of the woman I'm both desperate to talk to and desperate to avoid. "Sadie Winslow! What a pleasant surprise. Ava didn't say you'd be in town today."

"Oh." Sadie's gaze bounces between us, concern and annoyance flaring in her eyes as she steps closer.

I have no doubt the concern is for Gage. She may not have told Ava she'd be here, but Sadie is well aware of the week they had. Gage told me at the funeral how sorry Sadie was she couldn't be there to support Ava, but she'd been out of town on a two-week yoga retreat for work or something.

"I didn't actually tell Ava. I didn't want her to feel like she needed to come out and keep me company today. She should be wherever she is right now, not worrying about anyone else."

There it is—more proof that Sadie is nothing like her sister. That care and concern for someone else? I can't recall a time I ever saw Summer show that much emotion for someone other than herself.

How did I ever think the two of them were similar? When did Sadie ever show herself to be anything like her sister?

"She wouldn't have minded." Gage pulls Sadie into a hug and the spark of jealousy at their easy interaction makes absolutely no sense to me, not in a moment like this.

"And that's exactly why I didn't tell her."

Before anyone can say anything else, there's a crackle over the radios at both mine and Gage's hips. I immediately reach to lower the volume on mine so we can hear the words that come through more clearly out of just one radio.

"Can someone head over to the pie-making contest? There's apparently an argument about the final results."

Without checking with me, Gage lifts the radio to his lips and lets the dispatcher know he's on his way. "I'll catch you later, Reid. Good seeing you, Sadie." He squeezes her arm quickly before he walks away.

I'd almost think he planned it, except I know Marybelle is competing this year and I absolutely believe she'd throw a fit if she lost the pie-making contest like she did last year at the Fall Harvest Festival.

An awkwardness fills the space between Sadie and me, but neither one of us makes any move to walk away from the other. Her focus shifts to something beside us but my gaze stays trained on her.

In the setting sun she's practically glowing—the epitome of a woman who spent time out in the sun on a perfect summer day. From the hint of pink on her cheeks and shoulders to her hair thrown up in a messy tangle on top of her head, and all the subtle hints in her outfit to the holiday we're all here celebrating, I'm transfixed by her.

How did I miss her before?

She smiles and waves at someone to my left before bringing her attention back to me, that radiant smile quickly slipping from her lips. I so desperately want that smile to stay and be aimed my way, but I know I don't deserve it. Not with the way I've been around her.

"Hey." It's probably the absolute lamest thing I could say to her, but it's the only thing that comes out of my mouth.

"Hi."

That awkwardness is only growing between us, but she doesn't shift to move away, and I take that as a good thing.

"I wanted to apologize." I take a small step toward her, closing the large gap between us, wanting to make sure she hears my words in the crowd around us.

Her brows pinch. "Apologize for what?"

"Well, as you've pointed out a number of times, I've been an asshole."

Those lowered brows now rise in shock, and I can't help but chuckle. Considering the antagonistic interactions we've had, I shouldn't be surprised by her reaction.

"Gotta say, I didn't see that one coming," she murmurs under her breath. I doubt she meant for me to hear the words, but I do.

"Yeah, well, it's strange for me to act the way I have been around you, and I like to believe I can admit when I've been wrong. When it comes to you, I've been very wrong. There's no excuse for how I've treated you, so I'm just going to say sorry and ask if you can forgive me."

Her eyes narrow. I have no idea what she's thinking, but I wish I did. Is it distrust or something else swimming in her eyes?

It takes her so long, her scrutinizing gaze studying me like a complex math problem, I start to think it's a hopeless cause.

If I'm being honest, even if she does forgive me, I still don't know what I want. All I hear are Declan and Gage in my head telling me to go for it, but is this thing between us real or something imagined?

Sure, I've found myself thinking about her an almost endless amount since we first ran into each other on New Year's, but she's also the first woman in a while to not be swayed by my charm. Is it just the thrill of the chase drawing me to her?

"I forgive you." Her smooth voice pulls me back to the present.

"Just like that?"

"Yeah. You aren't the only one who's been rude, and while you may have deserved it, I don't normally give it right back. So, I'm sorry too."

Where Sadie's shocked that I apologized, I'm not surprised in the slightest that she did. In the short time we've spent together, I can tell that's exactly the kind of person she is.

With those simple words, the guilt that's been weighing heavy lifts and I can breathe easier again.

"Does that mean we're friends now?" I tease. I may not know if I want more with Sadie Winslow, but the only way for me to find out is to spend time with her, and now that we're putting our harsh ways behind us, maybe I can see if these feelings I've been having are real.

"I don't know if I'd go that far." She laughs, a little twinkle shining bright in her eyes. "But we could give it a try."

CHAPTER TEN

Sadie

"AREN'T YOU SUPPOSED TO be working?" I ask Reid an hour later as he continues to walk next to me down the crowded street.

This isn't my first festival in Ashford Falls—it feels like they have one almost every month—but it is my first Fourth of July here. Normally, I stay in Stonebridge Hollow and hang out with Madison and her family, but Summer asked me to come out to see her this year, and I couldn't say no to her.

Since Summer and Reid broke up, it's like she's pulled away from everyone back home. So when she reaches out wanting to spend time together—something that doesn't happen as often as it used to—I tend to drop everything to show up.

All relationships, no matter how strong they are, ebb and flow. I think I just figured, as adults, we'd be better equipped to handle those low moments.

Of course, while Summer and I started out spending the day together just the two of us, once a friend of hers showed up, I was ignored—exactly like New Year's Eve. Luckily for me, since spending time with Ava all over town, I've come to know a few more people.

I may have been walking around checking out everything by myself, but I wasn't lonely. At almost every booth and table someone I've come to know over the last few months was there.

"I am working. I'm keeping an eye out. Listening for dispatch calls." Reid bumps his shoulder against mine, eliciting a small smile from me. "We're in a relatively peaceful small town. The dustup at the pie baking contest is probably the only trouble we'll have. That, and maybe a call from Willow about the squirrel trying to steal something from her house."

"I'm sorry, but did I just hear you correctly? A squirrel?"

"Yep."

I wait, expecting him to elaborate, but when he doesn't I stop in my tracks, tugging on his arm to make him stop and face me. "You can't just say something like that and not explain. That's not normal."

"I wish I had an explanation, but I don't. Willow calls at least once a week about an attempted robbery by the squirrel living in the tree in her front yard. She once tried to get us to post an eviction notice for it."

Reid says this with such a straight face that I'm afraid to laugh at the ridiculousness of it, because that is ridiculous. But it only takes him a few more seconds to break, both of us laughing now.

It hasn't been long since we buried the hatchet—literally only an hour—but there's a peace and comfort between us. Almost as if we've been friends for a long time. That comfort has me seriously questioning everything I think I know about the man next to me.

According to my sister, he's the biggest of assholes. He's rude to everyone around him, only worries about himself, speaks badly about his family, and made it clear he never wants to get married or have kids. From the way Summer told it, he made her feel quite small and stupid for wanting both of those things, and that feeling was the final straw.

I'll be honest. When Summer told me how bad things really were between Reid and her, I couldn't understand how someone like Gage could be friends with him. But I just assumed I hadn't spent enough time around him to figure out the kind of man Gage was. Obviously Reid had tricked us all into thinking he was someone he wasn't, so why couldn't Gage have done the same?

But knowing Gage now? Hearing all the things he's done for Ava and how he supported her through one of the hardest times of her life? I can't understand it. Add in how close Ava seems to be with Reid at the Memorial Day barbecue, and I'm even more confused.

I started questioning it a little at Valentine's Day. I mean, he left at least forty dollars on the table when we only ordered drinks and the table was still filled. A person like the one Summer described wouldn't do something like that.

And at the barbecue, when he joked around with Max and kicked the soccer ball around with him, I couldn't help but question the truth about him not wanting kids of his own. It's not that I think everyone who's good with kids wants their own, but if he really thought children were a "scourge on society," he wouldn't have been so attentive to Max.

"You know, Willow is actually the person who orchestrated that Valentine's date from hell," Reid says as we both calm down.

"I mean, I wouldn't say it was that bad."

The look Reid shoots my way has both of us breaking again, and I can't help but sway a little closer to him.

"You're right, it could have been far worse." Reid smiles, his eyes lighting as he looks at me. "I might not have had you next to me."

"Reid…" I whisper, but nothing follows the single word, both of us lost in a trance, simply staring at each other.

I knew he was attractive the first time I saw him, almost six years ago. Summer wanted to introduce him to me before our parents, so she asked me to meet her at The Diner here in Ashford Falls. She was late, as usual, and I assumed she was coming with her boyfriend. So when Reid walked through the door alone, it didn't even cross my mind that he could be her boyfriend.

It was like a scene from a rom-com, the way everything around me disappeared and all I saw was this unfairly attractive guy walking through the door. I'd seen attractive men before, even dated a few, but Reid beat them all by a landslide.

He walked right up to the counter and started talking to the woman there, laughing and joking with her. I'd almost worked up the nerve to go talk to him when Summer walked through the door. She didn't even falter when she walked in, simply marched right up to him and pulled him into a searing kiss, almost as if she were staking her claim. The pang of disappointment I felt when I realized who he was made me feel guilty, especially after they came over and took a seat.

It was early in their relationship, maybe a month or two in, but I saw the way he looked at her—like she hung the moon. From that moment on, Reid was someone I didn't allow myself to think about. He was the guy in my sister's life. The guy she was supposedly falling in love with.

Now, though, I'm not so sure any of that is true.

Does that really matter?

He's still my sister's ex-boyfriend, and they were together for almost three years. Besides, up until an hour ago, we didn't even like each other. I don't know if I can say I hated him—though I wanted to—but loathe could definitely work.

The crackling of Reid's radio snaps us out of whatever moment we're having, the both of us taking a small step away from each other, before the sound of the dispatcher comes through. *"Fireworks will be starting in about thirty minutes. All officers should make their way toward the town center to help with crowd control."*

"I guess it's time for you to get back to work." My voice comes out soft, almost a whisper.

"What did I tell you?" His voice is just as soft as mine, as if he's just as worried about breaking this spell between us. "I've been working this whole time."

His brows pinch as his eyes bounce between mine. I have no idea what he's thinking, but he must come to a decision, because one second he's feet away from me and the next there's only inches between us. His next move is slow, giving me time to step away if I want, but I can't. This time when he brushes a piece of hair behind my ear and his fingers linger, I lean into the touch—into him.

His gaze drops down to my lips and then back up, and I don't even try to stop my tongue from slipping out to wet my bottom lip. I know I should pull away from him, stop this from happening, but I don't want to.

Just as he starts to close the remaining space between us, my sister's voice practically booms behind us. "Well, what do we have here?"

Reid pulls away moments before Summer pulls me into her side, her fingers digging into my hip with a biting pain. "The asshole of all assholes trying to take advantage of my baby sister. What. A. Shocker." She emphasizes the last few words, her tone mocking.

Reid's eyes slowly move from me to Summer, and when he speaks, his tone is completely flat, not an ounce of emotion is in his words. "Come on, Summer. If we're gonna throw stones, then let's at least be honest."

"I don't know what you're talking about." Her grip on my hip tightens, and if I weren't right next to her, I might have missed the hitch in her breath.

Why is she nervous?

"Summer," I whisper.

"You know what?" Summer asks before I can say anything else, releasing me from her grip and stepping forward. "You're right, let's be honest." Her voice rises, grabbing the attention of the people around us. "I've kept silent about the way you treated me for years. It's time the people of this town know who you really are."

Reid's eyes move from Summer to me. He's studying me like how I respond to this tells him everything he needs to know about me, and I wish I had the right answer.

"You're the one who broke us, with your ceaseless flirting with anyone who has a vagina and your never-ending judgment of every single thing I did. The way you made me feel small and stupid for wanting marriage and kids, and the way you spoke about your family…"

I know Summer keeps going, in the depths of my brain I hear her voice next to me, but it's like everything disappears around me and the only thing that exists is Reid. There's pain in his eyes, but he doesn't say or do anything. He just lets her continue to destroy his reputation, spouting what I now realize—without a shadow of a doubt—are lies.

I see the moment he gives up, a wall going up around him.

Without saying anything, he turns and walks away. The crowd around us, just as stunned by his actions as Summer is. But suddenly I get it, that's the man Reid is. Unwilling to make a bigger scene or degrade a woman for any reason—even though she probably deserves it.

"Where do you think you're going?" Summer shouts after him.

"Summer," I whisper, completely sick with myself. "Stop. Just stop."

She spins to look at me, disbelief pouring off of her, and suddenly it all clicks. Like a scene from a movie, all my major interactions with my sister run through my mind and I see the manipulative tactics she's used to make me side with her. Every story she ever told about Reid was a lie. He wasn't the person refusing to hold the door, or never saying please and thank you. He wasn't the one who didn't want kids and marriage.

It was all her.

My head falls forward, unable to look at her. There are a lot of words I want to throw her way, to hurt her the same way she hurts others, but I know it won't change anything. So instead, I follow in Reid's shoes and walk away.

I hear her shout after me, trying to save face, but I keep marching forward. There's nothing she can say right now to make me understand, and I don't know if there ever will.

AUGUST

CHAPTER ELEVEN

Reid

"YOU LOOK GOOD WITH a baby," Caleb hums as he takes the seat next to me. He reaches over, adjusting the pacifier in his daughter's mouth, before he sits back in his seat, apparently comfortable with me continuing to hold her.

I know my smile is tight, but it's all I have to give right now.

She hasn't arrived yet, but I have no doubt she'll be here to celebrate Ava's birthday.

I seriously contemplated not coming, but I knew Gage would never hear it. While he may understand why I want to avoid anything having to do with the Winslow women—even the one I still can't stop thinking about—he'd also tell me I can't let their possible presence keep me from doing the things I want.

Granted, it's not simply the idea of Sadie being here that made me want to stay away. I'm still hurt she thought I was ever capable of the things Summer said, but I understood how she might have thought that when we first ran into each other. I mean, I assumed she was just like her sister when I first saw her again, though I quickly realized Sadie wasn't anything like Summer.

It hurts realizing that, even as Sadie got to know me, she still thought I was capable of treating anyone like Summer described.

I thought she knew me better than that.

Five weeks later, and the town is just now starting to move on from the scene Summer caused at the Fourth of July festival. She may have wanted to turn the town against me, but all it did was prove exactly who the wronged person in our relationship was.

I'm sure it helped that I grew up in this town, but it's not like I've ever been the hometown hero. I made mistakes, but I also always owned up to them, and the people of Ashford Falls knew that. When it came to Summer Winslow, she hadn't just been rude and belittling to me, she'd done it to everyone she came across.

None of that stopped the gossip from running rampant, though. No matter how much this town knew everything she said was a lie, that didn't stop them from murmuring about how I let her treat me so poorly. That a tough guy like me, let a little thing like her, mentally and emotionally manipulate and abuse me for so long.

I don't think I realized it at the time, but I do now. All those snide comments and underhanded insults were indeed abuse. And if I'm being honest, I don't know what I would have done had I realized it sooner.

Not that it makes what the people of this town have been saying okay. I know it's not everyone, but I still feel let down by Ashford Falls, and it makes going out a little more tiresome than it used to.

But maybe that's my fault. As the saying goes, "expectations are premeditated resentments." If you don't expect anything from anyone, they can't let you down.

Caleb clears his throat, bringing me back to the moment. "What are you thinking right now?"

"I don't know if that's something you really want to hear." I scoff, focusing my attention back on the sleeping baby in my arms.

"Come on, man. It's not good keeping it all in."

"Are you a therapist now?" I lift my gaze to his and force a smile, wanting him to know I'm only teasing.

"No." He laughs. "But I did ace my psychiatry rotation in med school."

"And when was that? Ten years ago?"

"Only eight, thank you very much."

We both laugh, and I have to admit, this stupid little interaction makes me feel better. It shouldn't surprise me, but somehow that simple conversation lifts some of the weight I've been carrying around.

"For real, how are you doing?" Caleb sobers first, not letting me get out of answering his original question.

I avoid looking at him and bring my attention back to Fiona. There's something so calming about holding a sleeping baby, and I just want to soak in that feeling as much as I can.

"I don't know how to answer that question," I tell Caleb honestly. I wish I had a better understanding of what I was thinking and feeling, but I'm all over the place in that department.

"Well, maybe you break it up into smaller pieces. Instead of figuring out how you feel about everything that's been going on, just pick one piece of it." Caleb settles farther back into his seat, his attention drifting to the other side of the yard where his wife stands, talking to the principal from the high school. "Have you seen or spoken to Summer since the festival?" he asks, turning back to me.

"No, and there isn't a single part of me that wants to. I was done with her before this and I'm just as done with her now. Summer truly has no power over me."

"That's an interesting word choice."

I shrug, not really sure what I want to say to that. "Hindsight is both a glorious and frustrating thing. I recognize now just how much power I gave Summer. I mean, I let her dictate practically every aspect of my life, even when I completely disagreed with her. Even when I recognized how rude and disrespectful she was being."

When we were around other people she wasn't so blatant in her dislike of those around her, but behind closed doors? She was a completely different person. Maybe I let them slide because it meant I was the lucky one, the one she felt so comfortable with she could be honest about her feelings. Or maybe it was because I didn't recognize at the time how many of those comments were directed at me.

"I won't give anyone that kind of power again. Especially not someone like her."

"A narcissist?"

"I don't know if I've ever labeled it like that before, but that definitely fits." Fiona shifts in my arms, her brows scrunching for a second before she settles again.

"I wasn't around when you were dating her, so I only have the few stories I've heard to go on, but here's the thing." Caleb leans forward, resting his elbows on his knees. "The only way you hold on to all of the power is by not letting anyone into your life. And while I totally get it, I don't recommend closing yourself off." He reaches forward, brushing a gentle finger across his daughter's cheek. "I mean, I wouldn't have this little girl if I didn't give up some of the power. And when you find the right person, it's not a scary concept."

"How did you get so insightful?" I ask with a lift of my brows, my shock at his words more than obvious.

"Not in any way I'd recommend." The smile he offers me is both sad and reminiscent, and I know the next words he says aren't ones I want to hear. "Losing the man who raised you changes you in ways you'll never expect, but it also teaches you the value of people."

"I'm sorry, Caleb," I murmur. It's not the first time I've said those words to him, and I imagine it won't be the last time.

"I was blessed to have him for the time I did, and I was lucky I had the chance to say goodbye. In the grand scheme of life…" His words trail off and he stares out across the yard, this time to his kid brother.

I don't know if he intends to finish the thought, but I don't need him to continue. He had more time with his father than a lot of other people do. "That doesn't make it any less painful."

"No, it doesn't." His eyes come back to mine. "But it does make one more reflective."

I have no response to that, but Caleb quickly shows he wasn't expecting one. He stands from his seat, patting me gently on the shoulder to not disrupt his still sleeping daughter, and then he's off to join his wife.

My gaze drops to the innocent child in my arms, and I can't stop myself from thinking about what Caleb said. He didn't say anything groundbreaking—of course I have to give up some power if I want to have a life with someone—but seeing the direct result of what those words actually means has a different impact.

I may not have seriously thought about what my future looks like, but I always assumed I'd get married and have kids. Maybe that's partially because of society and what's portrayed in the media, but the idea of those things never felt wrong or like they weren't for me. I just didn't feel the need to rush down the altar—not that I feel like I need to rush now.

But I won't lie. Seeing all my friends partnering up does have that pinch forming in my chest more and more. Almost like I'm missing out by not having someone by my side—to lean on when I need and to support when they need.

I want what they have, and maybe, if I'm honest, I knew that before this conversation with Caleb. Maybe I knew I wanted that back on Valentine's when I wished I'd had more time with Sadie. When I wished my date had always been planned with her.

And just like I conjured her with my thoughts, Sadie Winslow walks through the back door, the woman from the bar on St. Patrick's Day by her side. It doesn't surprise me how beautiful Sadie looks in a simple summer dress with her hair pulled back from her face in a half-up ponytail. What surprises me is her unease.

Her eyes bounce around the backyard as she fiddles with the plate of brownies in her hands. I see her friend whisper something in her ear, and Sadie's eyes immediately fall to the ground before her.

I don't like the uncertainty, but I'm also not entirely ready to talk to her yet. I let my focus drift back to Fiona as she squirms in my arms, her eyes fluttering open. And proving mother's intuition is indeed a thing, Emily appears at my side.

"She's probably hungry."

"I guess that means I have to give her back," I tease, standing from my seat.

"Only if you want to avoid a screaming baby."

"Sounds like a good plan to me."

CHAPTER TWELVE

I THOUGHT ABOUT STAYING home today, and I would have if it weren't for Madison.

It's my own fault really—introducing Ava and Madison, two of the nosiest people I know, to each other. I know it all comes from a place of love and wanting the best for me, but it doesn't stop their meddling from getting annoying.

And boy do the two of them know how to meddle.

It started with Ava doing the subtle guilt-trip game. The one where she said she completely understood why I wouldn't be at her birthday party but also was really sad since it's been so many years since we celebrated birthdays together. But I still held strong, telling her we could celebrate next weekend, just the girls. It would be more fun that way, more intimate. We'd all have more time to spend one on one and she wouldn't have to feel pressured to entertain anyone.

I almost thought I got out of being here today. Dressed in my baggiest of clothes and prepping all the best junk food snacks for a couch rotting session, I wasn't ready when the knock came at my door. The moment I heard the sound I knew who it was.

Madison Hawthorne in all her glory.

She came barreling through the door, unwilling to hear the word no. It was abundantly clear she and Ava had worked together to make sure I showed up at the party today. And honestly? I love them for it.

An hour after Madison showed up, we were on the road headed for Ashford Falls. Only thirty minutes late for the party.

I'm not used to feeling so out of place, and even though I'm more than welcome in Gage and Ava's home, there's a discomfort being here knowing I hurt someone in attendance—even if it was unintentional.

I spent the last five weeks looking back at every interaction I had with Reid. Not just this year, but all the way back to the first night we met.

One of the things Summer said she hated most about Reid was his disrespectful nature. She talked about how every time they went out to eat, he never said please or thank you to any of the staff. Or how he never held the door open. Not for her, or for people who may have been only a few steps behind him. Or if there was ever an issue with the meal he ordered, while he didn't yell at the waiter to have it fixed, the tone he used was far harsher than necessary.

It was never anything big, but all those small things added up. At least, that's what Summer would say.

Looking back at the first meeting at The Diner, Reid was overly effusive in his gratitude to everyone around us. One might argue it was because he knew the people serving us— we were in his hometown—but when he came to Stonebridge Hollow to meet our parents, he'd been the same way. Every time I can remember being around him, he shared his gratitude in abundance—not just to those serving us, but to my parents and friends too.

I was already ashamed of how I'd treated Reid all year, but when I finally broke and told Ava everything, that shame quickly morphed to disgrace.

Ava had story upon story showing me exactly how wrong I was about him. He wasn't just kind to people around him, he was great at his job, he volunteered his time, he helped his neighbors, he rescued animals. He was literally the epitome of a good man.

Green flags left and right. There may be a red flag here or there—his lack of committed relationship being a key one—but who doesn't have at least one red flag? Plus, I'm not sure you could blame a man for not wanting to do the committed relationship thing after the shitshow that was Summer.

But then there's the truth about St. Patrick's Day.

It didn't matter how gentle Ava was when she spilled that truth. I wanted to crawl in a hole and never come out.

Gage and Ava may have been at that bar and they may have been with me in the hospital, but it was Reid who saved me.

It was Reid who followed me from bar to bar when he saw Madison leave.

It was Reid who paid attention to how I was acting and saw the moment everything changed.

If it hadn't been for Reid…

I shake my head, refusing to let my thoughts travel down that path. It doesn't matter what might have been, all that matters is what happened—and thanks to Reid, I was safe that night.

Walking out the back door, I can't stop my eyes from roaming the backyard, searching for him. I wouldn't be surprised if he skipped the party, but I'd hate it if I were the reason for him avoiding people he loves. My presence keeping him from being in the places he wants would never be okay, especially when I'm the one in the wrong.

Somehow, after Summer and Reid broke up, even though she kept living here and I kept visiting, Reid and I went three years without ever running into each other. And now, all of a sudden, we can't stop circling one another.

It would be just as the two of us are starting to get along—maybe even be friends—everything crumbles between us. Just as I'm realizing there might be something between us, something I'm willing to potentially hurt my sister over, I do something to ruin it.

Then again, would something happening between Reid and I hurt Summer emotionally or would it simply hurt her pride? And do I even care?

I'm still unsure if it's a good thing or not, but I feel like I'm finally seeing my sister for who she really is, and she clearly isn't a good person.

Just because you share blood with someone doesn't mean they have any right to walk all over you. I should have set boundaries with her long ago, but I was blinded to who she truly was because of my blind faith in her being my sister. I assumed she felt the same way about me—that she'd do anything for me the same way I would her. But I never would have lied about what happened with Reid, and I never would have treated people the way she so clearly has.

There's a high probability I need to cut her out of my life entirely, and after these last five weeks, I'm okay with that. Summer hasn't reached out to me once since everything happened, and every time I've reach out to her, it's all been about how horrible Reid was to her and the horrible things he said. Even knowing I was witness to all of it, she's still spinning the story to make her look like a victim.

Even more proof of just how wrong I've been about Reid.

The moment my eyes land on him I want to walk right up to him and apologize, but I can't force my feet to move. The fear and uncertainty consuming me. What right do I have to ask for his forgiveness? He doesn't owe me anything.

But, thinking about everything I've learned about him over the last eight months, there isn't some secret payment I need to make. He'll either accept my apology or he won't.

Maybe I should wait for his conversation with the beautiful woman to be over, but I just can't. I've finally worked up the courage to apologize, and I'm afraid I'll chicken out if I don't walk over to him immediately.

"Hmm," the woman hums. "Maybe you should take your own advice." She smirks as she steps away, giving me the opening I need.

"Reid, I'm sorry," I blurt the moment I'm in his space. "I wish I had better words than that. There's truly no excuse for any of it."

"Huh," he breathes out. "Those words sound awfully familiar." There's no censure in his tone, but there's no warmth either. It's almost like I'm a complete stranger to him, and I hate it. I think it hurts more than his anger might.

My eyes fall to the ground and I swallow, trying to keep my emotions in check. I don't know if crying in front of him would unintentionally manipulate him, and that's the last thing I want to do.

"Yeah, I'm definitely taking a page out of your book," I finally say, meeting his gaze head on when I've collected myself. "But…they were good words."

Reid doesn't say anything, but his shoulders drop away from his ears slightly, and I take that as my cue to continue.

"I was wrong to believe everything Summer told me, but

she's my sister and I assumed she'd never lie to me."

Reid opens his mouth but closes it quickly, shaking his head slightly. As if deciding whatever he wanted to say isn't worth it.

"I should have been a big enough person to think for myself, especially after talking with you on Valentine's Day," I continue when he doesn't speak. "If I'd paid the slightest bit of attention, I would have seen just how untruthful my sister was."

He nods his head, but doesn't say anything, and where I was hurt before, panic starts to take its place.

What happens if he doesn't forgive me?

"For some reason, we keep running into each other. After years of us going through the same motions and patterns, never seeing the other person once, we can't stop running into each other now," I whisper, taking a small step closer to him.

Reid shifts his weight and I see him visibly swallow, but he doesn't open his mouth to say anything.

"Don't you think that means something?" I ask, desperate to hear his voice.

He's quiet for so long, his eyes searching mine, I don't think he's going to respond, but then he does, I'm not sure there's any relief at hearing him.

"If you asked me that last month I probably would have said yes, but I'm not so sure anymore." There's sorrow in his tone, like it's causing him just as much pain saying the words as I feel hearing them. "I do forgive you, Sadie. I even understand how it could happen, but I don't know if I'm ready to give this another shot."

"Reid—"

"Just…" he interrupts, holding a hand out, silently asking me for one more second. "Just let me say this?"

I nod, swallowing the tears I feel building once again.

"I'm not saying we can't talk and be friendly when we happen to run into each other, because I don't see that stopping any time soon." He smiles, gesturing to the yard around us where all our mutual friends pretend not to pay attention. "But I'm not ready to pursue a friendship or anything else. Not right now."

He lifts his hand, as if wanting to tuck that wayward piece of hair behind my ear, but he quickly pulls back. Unable to say anything for fear of being unable to keep the tears at bay, I simply nod my head and offer him a tight smile.

The truth is, I completely understand where he's coming from. I may hate it, but I get it. So I won't fight him.

Without waiting for him to say anything else, I turn and make my way back over to Madison, asking her to please take me home.

OCTOBER

CHAPTER THIRTEEN

Sadie

THIS IS A HORRIBLE *idea.*

I shouldn't be doing this.

What in the world am I thinking?

The unease I felt walking into Gage and Ava's back in August is nothing compared to the fear I'm feeling now. In what world did I think showing up to a Halloween party dressed like this was a good idea? To a party I *know* Reid will be at.

"Stop panicking," Ava whispers at my side. "You look great."

"It's not about looking great. Anyone who knows what happened that night—"

"Meaning Reid," Gage mutters under his breath, interrupting me.

"I can't," I all but whimper as I spin around and start marching away from the house.

"Gage," Ava hisses before chasing after me.

I don't actually see it, but I hear her, and then she's there in front of me, gripping my biceps in her hands, and staring straight into my eyes.

"Sadie, you've got this." She shakes me slightly, and I

imagine she's trying to get the sense knocked back into me.

When she called me about the costume party Caleb and Emily decided to throw this Halloween, I immediately told her no. There wasn't a doubt in my mind that Reid would be here tonight, and even though twelve weeks have passed since we last saw each other, I'm still not ready.

But Ava convinced me it was a good idea. And she took it a step further, convincing me to wear the outfit I wore on that St. Patrick's Day bar crawl—with a few additions. The headband with a little green top hat and the green blazer being the biggest differences.

I questioned if it was smart of me to wear the same outfit I'd been roofied in, but only for a second. Yes, it was a traumatic experience that changed me in a lot of ways, but I'm also stronger because of it. And now, looking back at that night knowing the truth about Reid saving me, I don't want to give that asshole Kyle any power over me.

Wearing this stupid outfit tonight is my tiny sign to Reid that I know the truth and that I'm grateful to him—for far more than him saving me.

"No matter what happens with Reid, we're going to have a great time." She links her arm with mine, spinning us back toward the house. "Besides, we're here for Max. It's his first Halloween without his dad and they used to go all out for the holiday. And it's the last time we're going to see you until after Thanksgiving. Let's just forget everything else and have fun," she pleads.

"I know. I'm just…" My words trail off, and I can't stop myself from tugging at the hem of my leather shorts, as if they'll magically grow another three inches.

"Stop. You look hot. Right, Gage?"

"I plead the fifth," he responds immediately.

I know it isn't his intention, but the rapid fire response pulls a small laugh from me, and I'm grateful for it. Our eyes lock, and I know he's silently telling me everything will be okay.

It's not that I thought Ava lied to me, I'm pretty confident she and Gage have talked about everything, sharing their insights on Reid and me. There's a solid chance Ava pulled Gage into some meddling scheme to ensure Reid and I end up face to face tonight—just the two of us. I want that chance, but I won't force Reid into it.

Twelve weeks since I've seen him, and I've spent a lot of time thinking about what I want and what's truly healthy for us. I don't want us to keep hurting each other, no matter how unintentional any of that hurt has been.

If the last twelve weeks have taught me anything, it's that I miss Reid. I want him in my life, but I think the only way we can accomplish that is as friends. There's too much history to overcome and no matter how much I'm ready to put up boundaries with Summer, she's still my sister. I don't know if I'll be able to cut her out of my life entirely and I don't want to cause Reid more pain or strife should she ever show up when we're together.

I won't deny that there could be something amazing between Reid and me—I felt an instant connection to him the first time I saw him all those years ago at The Diner, and I felt it the moment I heard his voice on New Year's. I want to explore that, but I just don't think we can.

It's part of the reason I agreed to go fill in for a friend of mine at her yoga studio in Australia. Is it a little drastic for me to go all the way to the other side of the world to avoid my problems? Absolutely, but that's not going to stop me from doing it.

"All right," I say, taking one more deep breath. "Let's go."

I don't wait to feel the tug on my arm from Ava, instead I step forward all on my own, ready to face whatever waits for me inside that door.

- - - - -

ONE DAY I'LL LEARN never to doubt Ava. When she said Reid was doing just fine, she meant it.

I don't know what I expected when I saw him, but I definitely didn't think he'd walk right up to me with a warm greeting and a hug. At most I thought I'd get a brief wave—a simple acknowledgement that he saw me—but no. He walked right up in his Ferris Bueller costume with a big smile, greeting me just as affectionately as he greeted Ava.

He didn't stick around to make small talk, but it wasn't awkward between us either. Maybe being friends is an achievable goal for us? I don't know if it'll happen tonight, or even this year, but someday soon? It's a possibility.

I smile at the joyful sounds around me, not feeling an ounce of the discomfort I had before I walked in, and slip out the backdoor, needing a few minutes of quiet.

I love that I reconnected with Ava, and in turn made so many new friends this year, but all the laughing and talking is becoming a tad overwhelming. Just a few minutes in the stillness of the cool fall night and then I can go back in for a few more hours before I head home.

The sound of the back door opening has me turning to see who else has the same idea. I shouldn't be surprised when I see it's Reid. Something in the universe keeps throwing us together, why would it stop now?

"Hey," I say softly, not wanting to startle him if he hasn't seen me yet.

"Hey." He smiles. It's not even close to the large smile he had when he greeted me, but I'm glad it's a smile and not a frown. "How's it going?"

It's classic small talk, which isn't normal for us, but when I think about the fact our normal has been quite antagonistic…

I don't like this, but it's better than the harsh words we typically share.

"It's all right," I answer, turning toward the backyard. "How's everything with you?"

"It's good."

That awkwardness I assumed we'd have is in full force now. The silence stretches on between us, and even though I'm not ready to go back inside to the happy chaos, I can't stay out here.

"Did I hear correctly? You're leaving for Australia soon?" he asks so quietly I think I imagine it. But then he turns to face me and I know I didn't. Not with the furrowed brows and pinched lips.

"Um, yeah. You did." I shuffle my feet slightly, turning to face him. We're closer than I thought, but neither of us step away. "A friend of mine needed someone to fill in at her yoga studio while she's away at a retreat, and I figured why not." I shrug. It's a partial truth, but I don't think either of us are prepared for me to share the real reason I'm leaving.

"Gage said it's for a month," he whispers.

I swear he steps closer too, creating a little bubble around us.

"Not a full month. I'll be home for Thanksgiving."

"What will you do for Thanksgiving?" His eyes slide from mine, focusing on a piece of hair blowing in the gentle breeze.

"I'll be with Madison and her family this year," I murmur, hoping and wishing he'll reach to tuck that hair into place.

His eyes come back to mine, and I see the sorrow in them. He knows what holidays are like these days from his time with Summer.

My parents moved to Utah shortly after I graduated high school and rarely make the trip back to Stonebridge Hollow. Once Summer moved, they stopped making the trip entirely, and now they choose to go on a cruise for the holidays instead of spending time with their children.

I've never really understood it—how they went from being doting and loving parents to barely staying in touch—but I've accepted it at this point. Now I spend the holidays with people who care about me and have always shown that love.

"That'll be fun," Reid says, his eyes moving back to that piece of hair. "The Hawthornes were always very welcoming to me."

"That's just who they are." I'm barely able to get the words past my lips when his fingers brush my cheek as he finally tucks my wayward hair behind my ear.

Reid steps closer, eliminating those last few inches of space and I have no choice but to crane my neck back to keep my eyes on his. I see the moment his eyes move to my lips, and I don't even try to stop myself from running my tongue over my bottom lip.

"I know this is probably a bad idea," Reid mutters. "But unless you tell me to stop…" His words trail off, and when I don't say anything, but instead grip the sides of his sweater vest, his lips land on mine in a heated kiss.

I've fantasized about this moment more than I care to admit, but none of those fantasies come even close to the feeling of his lips on mine. Of our bodies pressed together.

"Sadie," he growls against me, pulling me closer, and deepening the kiss. His tongue glides across my bottom lip, and I don't hesitate to open for him.

A burst of laughter from the house pulls us both back to reality. We don't jump apart, but we do pull back, our eyes staying locked on one another.

"It may be a bad idea," I whisper. "But I don't care."

"Sadie—"

"No. Let's forget everything else, just for tonight," I beg, my grip on his sweater tightening. "Let's just be two people who randomly met and are attracted to each other. Two people who have amazing chemistry and want to explore that for a night."

His brows lift, but he doesn't immediately say no. "One night?"

"One night." I nod. "I leave for Australia on Sunday, and the chances of us running into each other again before the New Year is slim."

"What are you saying?"

"I'm saying we give ourselves tonight, work whatever this is between us out of our system, and then we move on. We be friends."

He hasn't pulled away from me and I take that as a good sign, but the longer he doesn't say anything the less confident I become.

"Okay," he whispers. "One night."

CHAPTER FOURTEEN

Reid

I KNEW THE SECOND Sadie walked through the door at Caleb and Emily's I wasn't going to be able to stay away from her. I've been trying like hell for twelve weeks to move on from her. To forget whatever this thing between us was.

There were a few too many nights spent out at bars, getting lost in the drink and trying to get lost in another woman. I'm not proud of it, but there were a few attempted one-night stands. Ones that never went further than the front door of their place.

No matter how much I wanted it, no one interested me. It was only the red hair, hazel eyes, and freckles of the woman pressed against my front door that did it for me. Only the quick-witted replies and caring nature of this beautiful soul that got my blood pumping.

I have no idea if one night is going to be enough, but if that's all she's willing to give me, I'll take it. At least for now.

"Reid," she breathes against me, her movements quick as she jerks my jacket down my arms.

After the thirty minutes it took to say goodbye, sneak out of Caleb and Emily's without anyone catching on we were leaving together, and driving to my place, I'm just as desperate to get my arms out of the sleeves and my hands back on her body. I need to feel her skin against mine. To feel her body pressed against mine.

The moment my arms are free, I pull my lips from hers, slipping down her body and onto my knees before her.

When Sadie walked into Caleb and Emily's in this green corset, dark leather shorts, and thigh-high boots, I wanted to drag her right back out the door.

All I saw was Sadie on St. Patrick's day, unconscious in my arms. It was like I was back in that room, my gut clenching with that same sick feeling of something bad happening to her.

But we weren't in that bar, and Sadie was happy and healthy. She was exactly where she was supposed to be surrounded by people who loved her. And when I let myself realize that, I recognized that I was proud of her for taking that power back. For finding a way to take back ownership of a night I imagine terrified her.

I want to ask her about it, but I'm afraid doing so will ruin the moment, that bringing up that night will do more harm than good. If it's something she wants to talk about, she will. If this is about her taking back power, then I have to give it to her. I have to trust that she's exactly where she wants to be, doing exactly what she wants to do. She hasn't done anything to indicate something different.

Her nails drag across my scalp and I can't stop the shiver from running up my back or the groan from leaving my lips. I focus my attention back on my mission—removing these sexy as hell boots.

Pushing her legs apart, I place a kiss to the soft skin on the inside of her thigh, letting my fingers tease as I pull the zipper down on her left boot. My movements are slow and methodical, drawing out the torture for both of us as best I can.

"Reid," she moans, her hips shifting, searching for pressure I so badly want to provide.

Not yet.

"Yes, sweetheart?" I ask as she steps out of her boot. There's a reverence to the nickname this time, one I hope she hears clear as day.

"I need—" Her words cut off in a gasp when I slide my hand back up her now bare leg, ghosting my fingers over the spot she wants them most.

"What do you need?" I repeat my movements on her other side, pressing a kiss to her inner thigh and following a path down as her leg is exposed with the lowering of the zipper on her remaining boot.

"You to touch me," she moans, her head falling back against the door.

"I am touching you." My hands coast up the backs of her legs, slipping under the hem of her shorts. I shouldn't be surprised when I feel the bare flesh of her ass—these shorts are far too tight for panty lines to be hidden—but I am. And I don't even try to stop my groan.

"You know what I mean," she pants, her eyes coming back to mine.

"No, use your words." I stand to my full height, towering over her for only a moment before I bend to her ear, whispering, "Tell me exactly what you want."

I see the goose bumps pebble across her skin and the desire to lick them burns so bright I can't help myself. I let my tongue travel up the side of her throat, sucking at the spot just behind her ear.

She starts to work at the buttons of my sweater vest and I

have no choice but to pull my hands away from her again, letting the sweater fall to the floor. I reach behind me, grab the collar of my shirt and pull it off in one smooth movement. I'm done having the feel of her skin torn from my fingertips.

"Tell me what you want," I repeat, pinning her hands against the door above her head when she tries to run her nails down my abs.

Her eyes heat as she squirms. I see the fear in her eyes, and for a second I think it's fear of me, but when the words finally slip past her lips so quietly I can barely hear them, I know it's fear of asking for what she wants.

Who the fuck has she been with before that's made her afraid to tell a man exactly what she wants or needs?

"I want your tongue on me," she whispers.

"Where?" I ask softly, dragging my lips across her exposed collarbone.

"Everywhere," she breathes out.

"What else do you want?" I switch my grip on her hands to her wrists, holding them in my left hand as I slide my right down her side, slipping it between our bodies to pop the buttons on her shorts.

"I want your hands on me," she swallows. "Your fingers in me."

"Hmm," I hum, slipping my hand down the front of her shorts, shocked at the feel of fabric beneath them. I don't let her thong distract me for long, not when I feel just how soaked she is for me. "Fuck. You're so fucking wet."

"Yes." The sound is more hiss than word, and I find I can't keep my lips off her.

It's a bruising and demanding kiss, one clearly showing my desperation, but I don't care, especially when she responds in kind, just as desperate as I am.

I slip my fingers under her panties and allow myself one swipe through her wetness before removing my hand from her shorts. Her wrists strain against my hold and I think about letting go, but I'm not quite ready to give up my control just yet.

I pull my lips from hers and press my body into her, letting her feel exactly what she's doing to me. Bringing my fingers to her lips, I coat them in her own wetness and when her eyes flare, I stop trying to hold myself back.

My lips are back on hers, and I swear I hear myself whimper at finally getting a taste of her.

Done messing around, I lift her by the backs of her thighs and make a mad dash for my bedroom.

I need to be inside of her now.

My knees hit the edge of my bed, and I turn, unwinding Sadie's legs from around my waist and lowering her from my hold to the floor. My lips don't leave hers as my fingers fumble with the hooks at the back of her corset. There's a moment of pure panic when I can't get even the first one undone, then I hear a soft chuckle from Sadie.

I pull back, instantly lost in the soft sound. "I haven't heard that nearly enough."

"Hmm," she hums. "We haven't been like this nearly enough." Her hand coasts over my abs and I instinctively flex at the feel of her skin against mine, eliciting another soft chuckle from her. "Show off."

"For you? Always."

Her eyes meet mine and the desire I see is no doubt a reflection of the need in mine. It's never been like this with another woman and if I think about that long enough, I might start to change my mind about "one night."

As if somehow reading my thoughts, with her eyes still

trained on mine, she trails her hand down to the button of my slacks and the moment her hand brushes my hard cock, all thoughts of stopping this vanish.

"You really don't need to. This"—she gestures to my bare chest—"is all awfully impressive."

I don't like to think of myself as conceited, though I know it can come off that way, but when you work hard to build muscle and stay fit, it's nice to know it's appreciated.

"And this"—I tug at the top of her corset—"needs to come off," I growl, desperately wanting to get my lips on every inch of her skin.

She smirks and grabs her hair, pulling it over one shoulder as she spins to expose her back to me. "Sorry, only way out is through."

The mischief in her eyes as she looks at me over her shoulder makes me feral. "Careful, sweetheart." I lean forward, pressing my lips to her ear. "I could always tear this thing to shreds."

She moans, and I force myself to focus, pulling away just enough to get started on the hooks running down her back.

The last hook releases and the corset falls to the floor, my attention now focused on the bare back before me. I've always considered myself a tits guy, but the smooth, toned back of the woman before me does something to me. I don't try to stop myself from peppering kisses along the newly exposed skin as I kneel behind her.

Carefully, I reach for the top of her shorts and drag them down her legs, leaving her thong in place and drawing out the torture for both of us just a tad longer. Instinct has me bending forward, biting and squeezing her ass cheeks.

Maybe I'm just a Sadie Winslow guy.

"Reid," she gasps, only for the sound to morph into a

moan as I spin her around to face me, pressing my nose into her soaked center as I gaze up at her, a groan rumbling through my chest.

"Fuck." The sound is drawn out and desperate, but I don't care anymore.

I am desperate for Sadie Winslow.

Keeping my eyes trained on hers, I grab the strings at her hips and tug her panties down her legs, stuffing them into my pocket before gently pushing her back on the bed. Without waiting for my direction, she scoots up the bed, her head falling to my pillows and her legs slide open just enough for me to clearly see her glistening center.

"You paint quite the exquisite picture." I lower the zipper of my pants and let them fall to the floor, stroking my cock once, twice through the fabric of my briefs.

"I'm going to give you everything you asked for." I push my briefs down my hips, letting them join my pants. "My mouth all over you." I crawl up the bed, holding myself over her. "On your pretty pink nipples." I lower my head and suck gently at one nipple before releasing it with a wet pop. "On your soaked pussy." I run a finger over her, stroking once before sliding in, another groan leaving my lips at just how wet she is. "But we have all night, and I can't wait to be inside you any longer."

Her hips rise as my finger slips free and she whimpers at the loss of contact. "Reid."

"I know, sweetheart," I whisper, pressing my lips back to hers as I reach for a condom from my nightstand. "I need it too."

The sound of the condom wrapper joins the sound of our labored breathing, and I'm just pulling the condom out when Sadie sits up, pushing my hand out of the way. Her eyes lift to mine, holding my gaze as she leans forward, taking my cock in her mouth. It's hot and slick, and I swear I almost come from that feeling alone.

Her head bobs a few times before I pull her off. "I need to be inside that sweet pussy. Now," I growl, sliding the condom on and pressing her back into the bed.

I settle my hips between hers, teasing her entrance with my cock before slowly pressing in, inch by agonizing inch. Her head falls back into the pillows, her eyes closed, and mine stay trained on her, looking for even an ounce of discomfort in any of her features.

When I'm completely sheathed inside her, I still, waiting for her eyes to open and meet mine. "You okay?" I whisper, pressing my chest into hers.

"Yes," she moans, lifting her lips to mine in a tender kiss. "But I need you to move."

I don't wait for her to ask again. I pull out and thrust back in, feeling her squeeze around me. It's ecstasy, being buried deep inside her. It's a feeling I know I want more of. One night with her isn't going to get this out of my system. I don't know if any length of time will.

I pull my lips from hers, lifting my chest enough to look down at where we're joined together, and I'm riveted by the sight of my cock disappearing inside her.

"Touch yourself," I growl. "Feel how wet you are. Feel my cock sink inside you."

"God, yes," she moans, when her hand slips between us, her fingers playing with her clit.

My balls pull tight and I know I'm on the precipice of coming, but I refuse to come until she does. Shifting to my knees, my ass resting against the heels of my feet, I lift Sadie's hips and power into her. She moans at the change in position and I feel her walls tighten around me.

"That's it, sweetheart. Let go."

Her fingers leave her clit as she presses her hands against the headboard, stopping herself from hitting her head. "Don't you dare fucking stop."

"Not in this life." I press my thumb against her clit, picking up where she left off.

Her eyes roll back and I want to demand they stay on mine, but then her thighs are shaking and she's screaming my name as she comes and I don't care that I don't have her eyes on mine. I thrust once more before my own release follows and I collapse on top of her, my hips shifting to ride out every last wave of her orgasm.

"We're doing that again," I breathe into her neck.

"We better."

- - - - -

WHEN I WAKE UP the next morning—only a few hours after finally falling asleep—Sadie's gone.

I shouldn't be surprised. She's always been a woman of her word. But that doesn't stop the twist of pain in my chest.

I was right.

One night wasn't nearly enough to get her out of my system.

NOVEMBER

CHAPTER FIFTEEN

Reid

"YOU DOING ALL RIGHT, Reid?" my brother asks, pulling my attention away from the television I've been staring at absentmindedly.

I know there's a football game playing, but I couldn't tell you a single thing that's happened since I collapsed onto the couch twenty minutes ago.

"Yeah, of course. Why wouldn't it be?" I smile, hoping he'll let it go.

Bryce and I have never been the closest, and I don't blame him for that. Sibling relationships generally go one of two ways when there's a nine-year age gap. Either you become really close or you don't.

Maybe if he hadn't gone away for college we'd be closer, but being around each other only on holidays for most of my formative years, we never really had a chance.

His brows pinch as he studies me and I'm not surprised when he pushes. "You've been quiet today, only really talking to the boys. You're normally a little more…" His words trail off as he searches for the right word.

"Vibrant?" his wife offers as she falls into the empty seat next to Bryce, her arm linking with his as she leans into him.

"Not the word I was going to use, but it works." He rests his hand on her knee, twisting to place a quick kiss to her cheek before turning back to me. "What's going on?"

They're right. Normally I'm the good-time guy, rough housing with my nephews and cracking jokes over dinner, but tonight I'm in a funk.

I've never really paid attention to the way Bryce and Roxanne interact with each other—or any of my friends and their partners—but lately, every tiny moment catches my attention. And with every easy moment, my stomach twists into knots.

I don't know why I do it, I've never talked to my brother or his wife about the details of my personal life—at least, not to the extent I do tonight. Sitting on this couch with them, I let everything about Sadie pour out of me. And I don't just start at New Year's Eve, I go all the way back to when I first met her.

I tell them about how I never looked at her as anything other than Summer's younger sister. Bryce chooses that moment to interrupt and tell me that's just who I am—I'd never look at someone else while in a relationship. The knot in my stomach loosens slightly at the knowledge he sees that loyalty in me.

I tell them how the second I saw her on New Year's Eve everything changed. She may have been my ex-girlfriend's sister, but now she was also this stunning woman I couldn't take my eyes off. How the more I ran into her the more I fell for her, even though I didn't know it at the time.

I tell them how when I finally realized it, she was already gone, quite literally, halfway around the world.

"Like, forever?" Bryce asks when I finally stop talking.

"No, not forever, but I think she's made it quite obvious

what she wants."

Roxanne leans forward, her mouth opening and closing a few times before she finally asks, "How so?"

"For one, she told me she only wanted one night—"

"Something you agreed to," Bryce interrupts.

"Shush." Roxanne swats at his arm gently before turning back to me, tilting her head, as if to say "continue."

"And she snuck out without a word. Not even a note."

Bryce and Roxanne share a look; a silent conversation being held between them. The knot in my stomach starts to tighten again.

The sound of pounding feet coming down the stairs causes all of us to turn at the abrupt entrance of my nephews.

"Uncle Reid!" Dale and Glenn shout at the same time, but the rest gets lost as they shout over each other.

"Whoa, one at a time." I chuckle. I may not be in a lively mood as my brother pointed out, but I've never been able to stay down long around my nephews.

"Dale said you wouldn't throw the football around with." My seven-year-old nephew steps between my legs, pulling my attention to him.

I shake my head, having no idea where that came from or how to respond.

"That's not what I said," Dale cuts in, pushing his younger brother out of the way. "I said you were going to throw the football with me first."

"All right, you two," Roxanne jumps in before I even have time to think of a response. "If you're going to argue about it, no one is going to throw the football with Uncle Reid." She stands from her seat, ushering both of them away from me. "Besides, we need to eat before there's any ball throwing. Let's go see if your grandmother needs help in the kitchen."

"But—" they both start.

"No. We can talk about it later. Let's go." She points in the direction they came, giving them her best *mom* look.

They begrudgingly march out the door, Roxanne following behind after she leans down, presses a kiss to my brother's cheek, and quietly whispers, "I think you should tell him."

Bryce watches her go, his eyes staying focused on the spot she disappeared long after she's gone. "Come on." He slaps a hand to my shoulder and uses me as leverage to lift himself from the couch, as if he's far older than his forty-two years. "Let's go out to the garage."

He doesn't wait for my response, already marching out the door everyone else just disappeared through.

By the time I make it out to the detached garage he's already pulled two beers from the fridge and popped the tops, leaning against an old workbench my father hasn't used in years.

"Should I be concerned we need drinks and to be fifty feet from everyone else?" I ask, taking the offered beer and leaning against the wall opposite him.

"I feel like I should apologize for the two of us not being closer." Bryce ignores my question and starts this conversation somewhere I never expected it to go.

"Bryce—"

"No. Let me say this."

I nod when he doesn't continue, letting him know I'll let him get out whatever he needs to say.

"You've always put in more effort than I have. Even before Rox and I had the boys, you always reached out wanting to know how I was doing and what was going on in my life. I may not have ignored you, but I also didn't give you much to go on." He pauses, his eyes bouncing between mine. "You're a good brother, and a good man."

I shift my weight from foot to foot, never one to accept compliments easily. "Thanks," I whisper. "I don't really know what that has to do with anything I told you earlier, but thanks."

"It's not the same, but Rox and I almost didn't happen."

"What?"

Maybe I shouldn't be surprised by that revelation, but I am. I've never seen two people more right for each other than Roxanne and Bryce. That may not be entirely true anymore, not after seeing Gage and Ava, and the rest of the group find their partners. But up until earlier this year, Roxanne and Bryce were the only example I had that I wanted to follow.

"We started in a similar fashion, not so much hate to love—"

"I've never hated Sadie," I interject, needing to make that clear.

"All right." Bryce chuckles softly. "Either way, Rox and I actually started out as friends, and then after one drunken night everything changed." His eyes get a glassed over, far-off look, as if he can clearly picture the moment happening right in front of him. "I was the one who snuck out and ran away like my life depended on it."

I know how this story ends—obviously—but when he doesn't continue, I start to get antsy.

"Remember when I took that semester abroad?" he finally asks.

"Sure."

"Do you remember how I left three months early?"

Now that he mentions it, I do. Mostly, I remember my parents being concerned. They didn't understand why he was leaving for another country when he'd planned on being home over the summer, especially since he wasn't going to be able to spend any of the holiday breaks with us that year.

"Rox and I went out with a bunch of friends on the last day of classes that semester. We had a few too many drinks, went back to her place, and…well, you get the gist."

Now it's his turn to shift uncomfortably, and I can't help but chuckle at the difference. I had no issues sharing with both of them what happened between Sadie and me. I mean, I didn't give them all the details, but I wasn't afraid to use the word sex.

"Yeah, I get it." I smile.

"When I woke up the next morning and realized what happened…" His words trail off and he shakes his head. "I don't know how to explain what happened. It was like one part of me was happy we were in that position. Happy to start exploring something deeper between us. I knew my feelings for her were becoming far more than friendly, but I hadn't actually admitted that to anyone, let alone myself."

"I completely understand that feeling," I mumble, more to myself than to him.

"Right." He nods. "The other part of me was terrified. What if we gave it a shot and ruined everything between us? What if she didn't feel the same way? And instead of facing those questions, I ran away and flew to another country."

"What—how…" I stammer, not knowing what question to ask.

"Roxanne didn't agree with pretending it never happened. We were friends," he reminds me. "She knew all about the semester abroad. So when I refused to answer her calls and texts, she showed up at my apartment in England, demanding I talk to her. And the rest, as they say, is history."

I open my mouth, but no words come out.

"You can play the what-if game all you want, Reid, but at some point you have to understand that unless you try, you'll never get the answer. Yeah, there's the terrifying what ifs, but what about the good ones? Like, what if she's the best thing that ever happened to you? What if it's amazing? What if she's the person you've been searching for? What if you lived through all that shit with Summer so you could appreciate all the good with Sadie?"

"What do I do?" I ask, but I already know that answer.

If I want to find out the answers to those questions, I have to fight for it.

CHAPTER SIXTEEN

Sadie

"I'M REALLY HAPPY YOU came home in time for Thanksgiving." Madison loops her arms through mine as we walk toward the front door of her parents' house.

"Me too." I smile at her.

Going to Australia was an amazing opportunity, and probably good for me in a multitude of ways, but I'm glad to be home and surrounded by people I love. They may not be my biological family, but I love them all as if they were.

The sound of toddling feet moving much faster than they should precedes the little voice of Jackson Hawthorne as he runs down the hall toward his aunt and me. "Sadie!"

I bend at the waist and catch him as his little feet get tangled up on the rug in the hall. "Hey, little man. Where do you think you're going?"

"No leave." His hands land on my cheeks as he squishes them together, and I can't stop the laugh from breaking free.

"I have to, little man." The words are muffled through my smooshed lips, but that doesn't stop him from understanding.

"Why?" He releases my cheeks only to cross them across his little chest, a pout taking hold of that precious face.

I could use jetlag as an excuse—I got home late Tuesday

night. Not that it would really be an excuse since I am exhausted, but the truth is, I don't have a valid reason to leave. I'm just peopled out, and that's not something a two-year-old would ever understand.

Like the hero his father is, Aiden Hawthorne strides into the room, saving me from needing to respond. "Come on, bear. It's time to get you ready for bed."

"No bed." He shakes his little head and starts kicking his feet, wanting to be put down.

I glance at Aiden and he gives his head a slight nod, letting me know it's fine to put Jackson down. As soon as I do, his little legs are running as he shouts for his grandma.

Madison and I chuckle, while Aiden shakes his head. We all know exactly what's going to happen now.

Ruby is the baby whisperer. She knows all the tricks to making Jackson think it was all his idea. Within the next twenty minutes Jackson will be in his pajamas, cuddled up with one of his grandparents, and falling fast asleep.

"You sure you're okay to get yourself home?" Aiden asks once we hear the hushed sound of Ruby's voice mixed with Jackson's.

"It's just down the street." I smile, a mix of annoyance and affection blending together.

There are very few people Aiden shows genuine affection for, and for the most part I'm glad I count as one of those lucky few, but sometimes his overprotective brother act is a bit frustrating. I know a lot of his concern stems from things he's seen in his past life in the FBI, but we're in Stonebridge Hollow, one of the safest towns in America. Literally, there was an article about it and everything.

"Just call or text when you get there, okay?" Madison steps forward, pulling me into a hug and cutting off her brother before he can say anything else.

"Yes, Mom," I tease.

"Get out of here and get some rest." She laughs as she playfully shoves me toward the door.

"Maybe I should just walk her home." Aiden's voice follows me outside, but I don't stop to look. I know Madison will stop him from following me entirely. Though I'm sure he's slipping on a coat and stepping onto the porch to watch me as long as he can.

When I started looking for a place to rent and saw this house, I knew I wanted it. The idea of being down the street from Ruby and Thomas—people who feel more like parents than mine currently do—made it the easiest decision. Even knowing Aiden is watching me like a hawk right now, I don't regret the decision.

A minute later I'm turning the corner onto the walkway up to my house, and even though I know he can't see me anymore, I still turn to look back in the direction I came, pulling out my phone and sending off a quick text to the Hawthorne sibling group chat.

Sadie: Made it home safe and sound.

The bubble indicating Aiden is typing pops up immediately, and I can't help the smile from forming.

Aiden: Inside?
Wyatt: Stop being such a worrywart!
Wyatt: Sleep tight, Sadie-bug.
Madison: Love you!

I tuck my phone into the pocket of my jeans and spin on

my heel, stopping in my tracks as soon as my eyes land on the figure sitting on my porch steps.

He stands, his hands shoved into his pockets. He's backlit by the porch light behind him, but I don't need to hear his voice to know who it is. "Sorry. I didn't mean to startle you."

"What are you doing here?" I'm frozen, unable to move in any direction.

I'm not sure when I expected to see Reid again. I knew it would happen, but I thought it would be much longer. While I can't say I was intentionally avoiding Reid, I wasn't planning on being in Ashford Falls anytime soon.

Reid closes the space between us, his eyes studying me. I'm not sure what he's looking for, but there's a comfort in him being so close. Something I didn't know I was missing.

"How'd you know where I live?" I ask before he can answer my first question, my tone quiet now that he's so close.

I want to reach out and touch him—to make sure he's really here and not just my imagination playing tricks on me—but I shove my hands into my coat pockets, forcing myself not to follow through.

When I snuck out of his house after that night—and morning—of mind-blowing sex, I instantly regretted it. It was a decision driven by fear and I'd been working like hell to stop letting fear run my life, especially after St. Patrick's Day.

But I was leaving for Australia the next morning and I didn't know what to do. I said one night, and Reid agreed. What if that had been all he wanted?

I couldn't take that kind of rejection.

Reid's shoulders fall and a small smile stretches across his lips as he lifts his hand and gently pulls my bottom lip from between my teeth. I didn't even realize I was biting my lip.

His words are soft as he answers my questions, his fingers moving to cup my cheek. "I wanted to see you. I missed you."

I melt at the words, leaning into his touch and soaking in the warmth of his skin against mine. I thought of this moment countless times while I was away. Imagining all the ways seeing each other again could have gone, this quiet moment, just the two of us, never crossed my mind.

"And I asked Gage for a favor, though I think I'm going to owe Ava a phone call in the morning." His thumb gently strokes back and forth against my cheek and I stop fighting my need to be closer.

"Ava?" I ask, taking a small step closer, tilting my head back and sliding my arms around his waist under his open coat.

"Yeah." He chuckles. "She's desperate to hear all the details."

"And you're going to give them to her?"

"Probably not," he whispers, his hand moving down my side and around me, pulling me in as close as he can get me. "But we'll still call her to give her the good news."

"What good news?"

"That we're giving this thing between us a real shot."

"Just like that?" I pull back slightly, needing to see his face.

"Well…" He bends, pressing a light kiss to my right cheek. "We could have a long drawn out conversation." A kiss to my left cheek. "Where we both talk about being afraid of the feelings growing between us." A kiss to my forehead. "Or we can jump ahead." A kiss to my nose. "Where we both admit we've spent the last month thinking about each other."

A kiss to my chin. "And we're ready to stop fighting ourselves."

He doesn't press a kiss to my lips like I assume, instead he holds where he is, his eyes bouncing between mine, silently pleading with me to put him out of his misery. He's not wrong. I've spent the last month thinking about a lot of things, the biggest one being how right everything feels when I'm with him.

Sure, there was some animosity between us at the start of the year, but if we'd simply gotten out of our own ways and actually paid attention, we could have been here sooner.

"Okay," I whisper. "We'll jump ahead to the good part."

"Yeah?" he asks quietly, almost like he's afraid if he speaks too loud I might change my mind.

"Well, the way I see it…" I rise to my toes, pressing a kiss to his right cheek, before pulling away completely. "If we're really doing this." I grab his left hand in mine, spinning to keep my eyes on his while walking backward toward my house. "Then we have plenty of time for the long, drawn out conversation."

The concern in his eyes disappears and he smiles, prowling toward me.

I laugh and run up the stairs, fumbling to unlock my front door.

His heat is at my back and his arms are around me before the key is in lock. "Just know," he whispers as he peppers kisses against my jaw and neck, "nothing has ever felt more real than this thing between us."

I get the door unlocked and push it open before spinning in his arms. "Ditto."

I know there's still a lot for us to talk about, but I'm thinking, in the grand scheme of things, they're pretty small.

And right now, all I want to focus on is the man in front of me.

DECEMBER

CHAPTER SEVENTEEN

Sadie

I WAKE TO A gentle squeeze and soft whisper from the man I've had the privilege of spending the last four weeks getting to know. I thought I knew him before he showed up at my door Thanksgiving night, but it's nothing compared to knowing him now.

When I joked about having a long, drawn out conversation, I didn't realize just how seriously Reid took it. Sometimes it feels like every conversation we have is just one long drawn out talk, and I love it. It's like we pick up right where we left off and somehow there's never any judgment.

Part of me thought it would take longer to broach the subject of Halloween, not so much what happened and why I disappeared on him, but my choice in costume. Ava told me to go for it, but I wavered almost up to the last moment. It felt wrong wearing pieces of an outfit that almost resulted in the worst night of my life, but it also felt important to take back control.

The thing that made me go for it was the realization that I wanted better memories, not just for me, but for Reid. Something traumatic happened to me, but something traumatic happened to him, too. We may not have realized it back in March, but there were feelings involved, and it couldn't have been easy for him to see me unconscious.

But, like with everything, we talked it out, and came out the other side better for it.

I know people probably find it odd how openly we talk to each other, but it's one of the things I love most about our relationship—and what an amazing relationship it's turning out to be.

Reid may have had significantly more sexual partners than me—and I know that to be true because he hasn't shied away from talking about them—but I've had more serious relationships. They may not have lasted as long as his relationship with Summer—which is still something I get funny feelings for when I think about it for too long—but they were serious nonetheless.

But none of them ever felt as strong as this one does. Even my longest relationship—one that lasted almost two years— doesn't compare to what Reid and I have after only one month.

We could argue that it's been longer than a month, but if you add up all the time we spent together before Thanksgiving I think we'd be lucky if it even equaled twenty-four hours.

Our time came down to a bunch of little moments here and there. Moments that, to most people, would be considered small, but to us, they were everything. We may have refused to acknowledge that in the moment, but looking back on it…I was falling for him the whole time.

"Merry Christmas, sweetheart," Reid whispers, his arms snaking around me as he pulls me close and nuzzles his nose into my neck.

The nickname that started out as an insult and has

morphed into something I never want to end pulls a smile to my lips.

"Merry Christmas, honey," I whisper back.

"You ready for today?"

"Don't remind me," I groan.

It's not that I'm not excited to be spending Christmas surrounded by so many people we love, but it's going to be a busy day.

"You're not excited?"

"I am. I just…" My words trail off and I lift his arm off me so I can turn to face him before letting it curve around my waist again. "It's going to be a long day. Maybe we should just go straight to your parents."

"And miss the morning with your family?" He tucks a piece of hair that's fallen from my nightly bun behind my ear. "No fucking way."

"I mean, they're not—"

"Don't even finish that sentence," he interrupts. "The Hawthornes are your family. You may not share blood with them, but they're your people, and that's all that matters."

I feel the tears well and I don't try to hold them back—not around Reid. He's the first person outside of the Hawthornes who has made me feel truly safe in showing my emotions, and letting the tears show now feels like honoring that connection with him.

"Thank you."

"You don't have to thank me, sweetheart."

"Maybe I don't need to, but I want to." I shift, pressing my lips to his and when I pull back, the heat in his eyes tugs me back in. "Do we have time for this?" I whisper as he moves us, his back to the bed and my legs straddling his hips.

"Does it matter?" His hands coast up my sides, slipping

under the T-shirt I stole from him weeks ago and finding my pebbled nipples almost instantly.

"No," I gasp, rocking against him. "But we should hurry."

"Oh, sweetheart…" He smirks, his tone telling me exactly what he thinks about that.

Doing the complete opposite, Reid sits up and slowly lifts the shirt over my head, tangling my wrists in the fabric above my head before flipping our positions.

"You know better than to tell me what to do," he murmurs directly in my ear before starting a torturously slow journey down my body, licking and kissing practically every inch of my exposed skin, stopping only when he reaches the apex of my thighs.

I know I'm soaked—already on the edge of orgasm—but when it comes to this man, he knows my body like no other. It's like he's drawn a map and memorized every road and valley, knowing exactly which paths to take. He never misses and the journey is always worth the ride.

"Reid," I beg, needing him to touch me.

"Yes, sweetheart?" His fingers slip in the side of my panties, pulling them down my legs.

Never one to pass up the opportunity to make me use my words, he stills once I'm completely bare before him. His breath plays against my skin and I can't help but shift my hips, hoping the movement will give me the friction I need most.

"Please, Reid. I need you."

"What do you need?" His eyes stay glued on mine as he swipes one finger through my soaked center.

My back arches at the contact and I lose all focus. "Reid. Pl-please," I stammer.

"All right. I've got you."

He slides two fingers in, curving them up just as his tongue lands on my clit, and I'm gone. All thoughts other than how good this feels disappear. The only thing that exists is Reid and me in this bed. Him bringing me pleasure in a way no one ever has before or anyone ever will.

Reid Alexander is it for me.

It's not just the moments like these. It's every second with him.

When we're together I feel safe and seen. Like, no matter what happens in the world, everything is going to be okay.

"Reid," I moan, my wrists still bound in the T-shirt above my head, my heart hammering in my chest.

"Let go, sweetheart," he murmurs against me, and as if my body has no other choice but to listen, I fall over the edge.

- - - - -

"I'M GLAD YOU BOTH could make it," Thomas, Madison's dad, says hours later as we get ready to leave for Ashford Falls.

"Of course. Thanks for switching things around so we could all be together this morning," Reid offers as he helps me into my coat.

"Are you kidding? Ruby was so happy with the change. It meant Jackson woke up here for Christmas morning."

I don't even try to stop the laugh from slipping free. I can imagine just how excited Ruby was at the prospect.

"Merry Christmas, Tom." I pull him in for one final hug.

"Merry Christmas, sweet girl. We'll see you soon, both of you." His eyes meet Reid over my shoulder and the smile he offers tells me exactly what he thinks—he likes Reid quite a bit.

"Absolutely." Reid places his hand on the small of my

back. "Tell everyone goodbye for us," he says gently before we turn, heading for his truck.

"You sure you're ready to leave? We can stay a bit longer."

"No, it's good to go while everyone's distracted." I hop into the passenger seat, and before I can do anything else, Reid's there, buckling my seat belt and pressing a quick kiss to my lips.

"If you're sure."

"Positive." I smile, reaching up to brush the hair from his forehead.

"All right," he whispers, taking his time to pull away from me. "Let's get out of here."

CHAPTER EIGHTEEN

Reid

"OH, IT WAS SO good to see you again." Roxanne's arms wind around Sadie, pulling her in for a tight hug. One that has them swaying back and forth.

"All right, Rox. Let her go." Bryce laughs, trying to pull his wife away.

"I don't want to." Her arms loosen and when she pulls away there's a literal pout on her lips, making all of us laugh.

Bryce tugs her into his side, pressing a light kiss to her temple. "It's not like you won't see each other again."

"I know, but still."

"I had a really great time tonight." Sadie smiles, slipping her arms into the coat I hold behind her.

Sadie's met my family once before, near the end of Summer's and my relationship, but I know she was nervous for tonight. No matter how much we talk about it, there's still a small cloud over us. I was with Summer for almost three years. Not only was it my longest and most serious relationship—one we all thought would end in marriage—but it was with her sister.

There's not a single part of me that looks back on that relationship as anything other than one I should have cut off sooner. I don't miss a single thing from my time with Summer.

When it comes to this relationship with Sadie, it feels light years different. Everything with Sadie feels like more. There's more comfort, more confidence, more laughter, more gentleness…more love.

I haven't told her those three words yet, but I feel them every day. My love for her grows leaps and bounds every time we're together, and it proves over and over how wrong Summer and I were together.

There's no comparison between the two of them. And while Sadie may say she knows that, I think tonight helped drive that point home. Especially after the blow-up that happened when Sadie told Summer about us.

We talked about it and decided while it'd be better for Sadie and Summer to meet one-on-one, I didn't want her to face Summer by herself. I know Sadie hoped Summer would prove us wrong, but we both prepared for the worst, and unfortunately, Summer was exactly who we expected her to be.

Sadie tried to get Summer to come out to Stonebridge Hollow, but after a week of Summer continuously bailing at the last minute, Sadie decided a phone call would have to do. I sat next to her on her couch and held her hand through the entire conversation, which went exactly like I imagined it would.

Everything was about Summer and how horrible we were treating her. How unbelievable it was that Sadie could stoop so low as to be with me. Sadie let her rant for a solid five minutes before she finally interrupted her and calmly told her to keep it to herself. There was nothing Summer could say or do that was going to tear Sadie and I apart.

Summer hung up without a goodbye and the two haven't spoken since. Though, Sadie still sends a text every week telling her sister she loves her and hopes life is treating her well.

I have no idea if the two of them will ever have the kind of relationship Sadie wishes they could, but I know I'll never let her regret choosing me, because I sure as fuck don't regret choosing her.

Tonight could have gone a few ways, but I know Sadie's biggest concern was that everyone would look at her as a duplicate of Summer, but that wasn't even close. If I'd been able to get my head out of my ass back in January, I would have seen that just as quickly as my family did.

The moment we walked in, it felt like Sadie had always been a part of our family, and even though it's too soon, I'm already eager for the day I get to make that officially true.

"All right. We're getting out of here before things get more emotional," I tease, slipping on my own coat before opening the front door.

"What are you talking about?"

"Love of my life, you're tipsy and with that tends to come tears," Bryce reminds Roxanne as gently as he can.

"That's not true." Her words shake slightly as tears start to well.

"Baby." Bryce smiles, cupping her cheek and stroking lightly.

A month ago, that little show of affection had my stomach twisting into knots. Today I feel nothing but happiness.

Slipping my hand into Sadie's, I gently tug her out the door. There's no reason for us to stick around for the mushy moment they're about to have. I love my sister-in-law, but Bryce is right. They may be the happiest tears in the world, but Roxanne and drinking means tears, and nothing will stop that.

"It's snowing." Sadie stops in the middle of the yard, her arms held out wide as she looks up at the sky and spins slowly. Her tongue peeks out, catching snowflakes, and I'm completely mesmerized by the sight.

How did I end up here with this amazing woman by my side? What did I do to deserve this feeling growing in my chest?

Sadie turns, and the smile on her face is radiant. "What?" she asks when I don't move from my spot at the bottom of the porch stairs.

"You're beautiful," I whisper, finally moving toward her. The second she's within arm's reach, I pull her into me, my arms tight around her body.

"You're pretty handsome yourself." Her arms wind around me as she presses her body to mine, her head tilted back to look at me.

I get lost looking in her eyes, and I'm not sure I mean for the words to slip out, but I'm not mad when they do. "Nine holidays falling."

"What?" Her brows pinch and I wouldn't be surprised if she genuinely didn't hear me with how soft the words were.

"Nine holidays is all it took to fall in love with you."

There's a quick inhale of breath as her eyes bounce between mine. I'm not sure what she expects to find, but I know the only thing shining through is my love for her.

"Well..." She smiles, her arms squeezing once. "Technically, it was eight holidays and a birthday party, but yeah." Her eyes stay locked on mine. "Nine holidays falling, indeed."

"I love you, Sadie Winslow," I tell her, wanting to make

sure she knows beyond a shadow of a doubt what my feelings are. "I don't know what the future holds, but I know I want you by my side. That might be a lot for only a month in—"

"I'd say we're almost a year in," she interrupts. "But even if we're not and we're only counting one month, I feel the same. You're my safe place, and I don't think I'll ever find another. I don't want to find another."

"Well then, I guess we've got a lifetime of holidays, don't we?"

"Yeah, we do."

NOT DONE YET?

Neither was I.

Scan the QR code below to get your copy of an exclusive bonus scene.

If you'd like to stay up to date on all things Erin Graves, including new releases, bonus content, behind the scenes, giveaways, and more, be sure to sign up for my newsletter.

ACKNOWLEDGEMENTS

The number of times the plot for Reid and Sadie's story changed…sometimes I'm a little surprised this story made it to this point.

That said, I think the first person I need to thank this time is Anna. You were with me from the very first concept to the very last draft of this book and while I know it was a rollercoaster of emotions for you, your support truly means the world.

To my alpha readers, as always, this story wouldn't be what it is today without you. Kelly and Paige, thank you.

To my beta readers, your comments constantly give me life and new motivation to keep going on this crazy author journey. Emily, Sarah, Sydney, Mary, and Annelise, from the bottom of my heart, thank you.

Caroline, my amazing editor. Maybe one day I will figure out where a comma goes (let's not hold our breath though, all right?), but until then, you're my hero.

Dana, my magnificent cover designer. I gave you the absolute bare minimum and you gave me the perfect cover for this story.

Alex, my amazing, talented sibling. You blew the character art for this one out of the park! Seriously. It's beautiful and perfect and everything I wanted for Sadie and

Reid.

You. I'll say it every time, but this story wouldn't exist without your continued support. Whether you bought a copy or read on Kindle Unlimited, without you these words would mean nothing. So thank you for reading, for commenting, for sharing, and every other thing you do to support me.

And finally, as always, my husband. You are a constant inspiration for both my writing and my life. I'm lucky I get to call you mine. Thank you for always pushing me and being by my side.

CONTENT WARNING

Please note that some of these trigger warnings are discussed in detail and on-page, though none of the scenes they are discussed in are long. That being said, please take care of yourself first and foremost.

- Depictions of involuntary drug use (roofies) (on page)
- Mentions of mental and emotional manipulation/abuse (in the past/off-page
- Death of a side character (mentioned briefly)

ALSO AVAILABLE FROM
Erin Graves

The Love in Ashford Falls Series
Shuttered Hearts
Unexpected Love
Hidden Vows

Novellas
Nine Holidays Falling

ABOUT THE AUTHOR

Erin Graves writes small town contemporary romance novels with a lot of heart and a touch of spice. She's a wife, cat mom, author, and sometimes crocheter. She was born and raised in Maryland and now lives in Pennsylvania with her husband and two cats. She started writing in high school but stopped when she thought she could never be a published author. Fifteen years later, her first novel was published.

STAY CONNECTED

You can find Erin Graves in all the usual bookish places…

Website:
eringravesauthor.com

Instagram:
instagram.com/author.eringraves

Facebook Reader Group:
facebook.com/groups/eringravesreadergroup

Goodreads:
goodreads.com/eringravesauthor

BookBub:
bookbub.com/authors/erin-graves

Amazon:
amazon.com/author/eringraves

Pinterest:
pinterest.com/authoreringraves